Matchmaking Christmas

Books by Toni Shiloh
from Bethany House Publishers

In Search of a Prince

To Win a Prince

Hearts on the Fly

LOVE IN THE SPOTLIGHT

The Love Script

A Run at Love

The Nature of Love

NOVELLAS

You Make It Feel like Christmas

The Christmas Catch

Matchmaking Christmas

Matchmaking Christmas

A Sweet Holiday Romance Novella

TONI SHILOH

BETHANY HOUSE
a division of Baker Publishing Group
Minneapolis, Minnesota

Published by Bethany House Publishers
Minneapolis, Minnesota
BethanyHouse.com

Bethany House Publishers is a division of
Baker Publishing Group, Grand Rapids, Michigan

Printed in the United States of America

Library of Congress Cataloging-in-Publication Data
Names: Shiloh, Toni author
Title: Matchmaking Christmas : a sweet holiday romance novella / Toni Shiloh.
Description: Minneapolis, Minnesota : Bethany House Publishers, a division of Baker Publishing Group, 2026.
Identifiers: LCCN 2026017169 | ISBN 9780764246869 paperback | ISBN 9781493455454 ebook
Subjects: LCGFT: Christmas fiction | Romance fiction | Novellas
Classification: LCC PS3619.H548 M38 2026
LC record available at https://lccn.loc.gov/2026017169

Cover design by Peter Glöege, LOOK Design Studios

The author is represented by Rachel McMillan.

Baker Publishing Group publications use paper produced from sustainable forestry practices and postconsumer waste whenever possible.

26 27 28 29 30 31 32 7 6 5 4 3 2 1

To the Author and Finisher of my faith.

Prologue

Malea

FIRST DAY OF FIFTH GRADE

My blue jumpsuit looks so good! I grin at my reflection in my floor-length mirror. Dad paired blue bows around my Afro puffs, and it ties the whole look together. It's the perfect first-day-of-school outfit.

"Malea! Let's go," Dad yells. "You already missed the bus."

Oops, but I had to make sure my clothes were perfect. He's always rushing me because he has a lot of work to do. I grab my *Little Mermaid* backpack and matching lunch box.

"You brushed your teeth, right?" Dad asks when I step onto the first-floor landing.

I roll my eyes. "I'm not a baby. Of course I brushed my teeth."

"I know, squirt." He pats my head and then opens the front door for me. "Still gotta ask in case you forget."

Whatever. I trudge out the front door but smile as I take in Dad's blue truck. It's great for hauling the Christmas trees and firewood he sells. Though it's only August, Christmas will be here before we know it. I've already figured out what I want for a present, but I don't know how to ask Dad for it.

How do I tell him I want a new mom?

No, my mom's not dead, but she might as well be. She left us six years ago, and if it weren't for the picture on my nightstand, I honestly wouldn't remember what she looks like. She rarely calls, and I haven't seen her in a few years.

I want a mom who will watch my favorite movie with me (a.k.a. *The Little Mermaid*, the live action version). I want a mom who can do my hair, and not the two Afro puffs Dad does every day because he's too busy to figure out how to do anything else. I want a mom who will go shopping with me. Who I can ask about girl stuff. Most importantly, I want a mom who will stay and love me and love Dad. Is that too much to ask for?

God, please, please, give me that type of mom.

Dad pulls up in front of Holly Elementary, and I unbuckle.

"I'll see you later."

"'Kay. Bye."

"Love you, squirt."

I glance over my shoulder before I close the door. "Love you too!"

Dad smiles, and a part of me warms. He rarely smiles, but when I tell him *I love you* he gives the biggest grin. It's his best feature, and I hope one day he'll use it more.

I wave and head into school. I see some of my friends and squeal with excitement.

Julie walks over to me and motions to my clothes. "Great jumpsuit."

"Your skirt is cute." It has little puppies all over it.

"Oh my gosh. Malea, look." Julie points over my shoulder.

I turn around and freeze. A new girl is walking down the hall wearing my exact jumpsuit. Her hairstyle is different though. It's in some kind of twist out, which actually looks cute.

Her gaze shifts to me, and I can tell the moment she discovers our outfits match. She scans me all the way to the blue Chucks on my feet—which match the ones she's wearing—and back up to the blue bows in my hair.

She grins and walks over to me. "Guess we're twinning, huh?"

"I don't know. What kind of backpack do you have?" I ask.

"Oh. *Little Mermaid*."

Julie gasps.

Before I can decide if I'm happy or upset about this stranger dressing exactly like me, Ms. Donahue walks toward us.

"Girls, don't you think you should be in class?" She raises a pointed brow.

We're not supposed to loiter in the hallways, but I didn't get to hang out with Julie all summer since she went to Texas to visit her grandparents.

"I'm new. Do you think you could help me?" New Girl asks Ms. Donahue.

"Oh, are you Kyleigh Parker?"

New Girl nods.

"You're in my class with Malea." She points to me.

New Girl is in my class. And though I want to like her, I'm not sure I can.

Kyleigh

SEPTEMBER

Ms. Donahue just assigned us partners for our first project—a report on a local hero.

I stare at the girl who I'm hoping will become a friend. I've been friendly all last month, but she hasn't warmed up to me yet. Moving to California means I don't know anyone here, and I'm hoping for at least one really good friend.

"So who do you want to do the report on?" I ask.

"My dad. He runs the tree farm, and everyone loves coming to our place during Christmas."

"A tree farm?" My jaw drops. "That's amazing! It must be like a fairy tale, living at a tree farm."

"I do love it." Malea nods slowly. "But who do you want to do a report on?"

"My mom. She just opened a candle shop."

"Wow. She's a boss babe?"

I giggle. "Yep."

"What does your dad do?" Malea asks.

My chest gets tight. I hate telling people, but something lets me know Malea would understand. "I don't have one. He died when I was a baby."

"I'm so sorry. I don't have a mom. Well, I do, but she left me six years ago." She shrugs like it's no big deal, but her bottom lip is shaking. "It's just me and my dad."

"It's just me and my mom," I say.

"So we do a report on both of them?"

"Let's." We shake hands, and the tightness eases. She does understand.

Malea
OCTOBER

I run toward Kyleigh as soon as I see her in the hall. "Hey! What did your mom say?"

Ever since our project last month, we've been best friends. Kyleigh and I click better than any friend I've had before. But we've yet to plan a playdate—Why do parents use that word? It should be for toddlers—because our parents keep coming up with excuses.

"No." Kyleigh frowns. "I don't know why she won't let me hang out. It doesn't feel like we're as busy as she says."

"I get it. Dad's always at the tree farm, so he's actually busy, but I was still hoping something would change."

"Me too," Kyleigh mumbles. "I wonder what we can do to change their minds."

"We'll brainstorm and figure something out."

She nods.

"Girls, get to class," Ms. Donahue calls from down the hall.

We sigh but head straight for our classroom. Once we're inside, we hang our backpacks on the wall hooks and put our matching lunch boxes beneath our backpacks. We're not tablemates because Ms. Donahue says we talk too much.

"Talk to you at lunch?" I ask.

Kyleigh nods.

Kyleigh
LATE NOVEMBER

I place my *Little Mermaid* lunch box on the table just as Malea places hers on it and sits across from me.

"Why is reading so boring?" Malea grumbles. Her twin Afro puffs are fire. She looks cute today.

"It's not," I reply. "But *Treasure Island* is a boring story."

Malea wrinkles her nose. "I don't know why you like to read, Kyleigh."

"Borrow some of my books and you'll understand." I have a mini library in my room that includes all of my most prized reads.

She sighs and takes a bite of her turkey sandwich instead.

I open my bento box and offer her a pinwheel. Her dad makes her the same lunch every single day. Turkey sandwich, sliced apples, and baby carrots. Despite asking for a different meal, he insists on doing the same thing.

Boys.

After eating the pinwheel, she looks at me. "I wish I had a mom at home like you do."

"Same. Well, reverse." I shake my head, my thoughts jumbling up. "I wish I had a dad at home like you."

"He's really handy around the house." Malea's face brightens at the thought. "And living on a tree farm is the best when Christmas comes."

"Do you have more than one Christmas tree in your house?" I ask. We love Christmas. Mom and I always go all out to decorate.

"Well, no, but maybe because there are so many outside."

That makes sense. "My mom loves Christmas. She usually puts a tree in our living room. Miniature trees in our bedrooms. And I think she's planning on getting one for her store."

"I bet your place smells dreamy all the time." Malea continues munching on her sandwich.

My nose wrinkles. "Sometimes she makes a scent that tanks. Once one smelled like sewage."

Malea pretends to gag, and we both laugh.

"Wouldn't it be awesome if our parents got together?" Malea asks.

"They'd have to meet first." Despite our brainstorming, we haven't managed to have a meetup outside of school.

"But our parents are always busy," Malea cries.

She's dramatic, but I love her. I simply nod and keep eating.

"Isn't there a way we could force their hand?"

I consider the question. "Maybe?"

Her eyes widen. "Oh! I got it. It's def a risk, but . . ."

"But what?" I ask.

"What if you go to my house and I go to yours? We'll switch bus stops, so that you get off at my stop and go to my house, and I'll get off at yours and go to your place. Then they'll have to switch us back in order to take us home. They'll meet, fall in love, and then boom!" Malea makes an explosion motion with her hands. "We'll be sisters."

Huh. I give her idea some thought. "That's actually next-level genius."

"Right?"

"What if switching places isn't enough? What's to keep them from ignoring each other again?" Because, hello, they still haven't met.

"Hmm." Malea taps her chin. "Great question. We want them to keep seeing each other. We *need* them to."

The idea of a dad *and* a mom is exciting. I'm practically vibrating in my chair. How do we ensure our parents keep running into each other? I think for a moment, then get a spark of inspiration.

"What if we sign them up for the Christmas events?" Our town has tons of things to do during the holiday season, and my grandmother has been telling me all about them, trying to convince me how much fun I'll have living here. I never imagined Northern California would have a Christmas town because the movies are always showing places in the East. But Holly is beautiful.

"Oh yeah! Like the snow-family contest," Malea says.

"Or the gingerbread contest."

"And the Christmas scavenger hunt." Malea smiles. "Brilliant, Kyleigh."

"Do you think those ideas are enough?" I ask.

Malea tilts her head. Then her eyes go wide once again. "What if we get them to help out with the Christmas concert?"

"Yes!" I barely muffle a squeal in time. A quick glance toward the lunch monitor shows my high-pitch noise went unnoticed. Jimmie is throwing food at the third-grade table and has the lunch monitor trying to rein him in. It's a daily occurrence.

I turn back to Malea, heart pounding. "So we're going to do this? Get them together?"

"Definitely." Malea holds out her hand. "Handshake?"

"Handshake."

We slap hands, swing back to tap knuckles, fist-bump top, then bottom, then back to the front, before miming an explosion. We fall over giggling, but no one even bothers looking at us. Everyone else at lunch is involved in their own conversations. No one knows we just cooked up a scheme to get our parents to fall in love so that we can be sisters and have a real family.

I close my eyes and bow my head.

Dear God, it's me, Kyleigh. Could you please see that our plan works? Mom really needs a partner, so she won't be so lonely, and I know Malea's dad is lonely too. I don't need any Christmas presents, just a family. Please help us make it work out! In Jesus's name, amen.

I open my eyes and grin at Malea, who has her head bowed too. If we're both praying, God's gotta hear us, right? Pretty sure I learned that at Sunday school. But I'll keep praying every day until He does.

Chapter *one*

Regina

Hot cocoa and a Christmas movie sounds like the perfect way to end the day. Everything that could've gone wrong went wrong, and now I simply want to curl up with my favorite person and let some Christmas movie magic work like Calgon and take me away. But first, I need to make it through my front door.

Moving back to my hometown of Holly, California, has been an adventure. We're in the Sierra Nevada mountain range, about a two-hour drive west of South Lake Tahoe. The rugged beauty has always held my heart, even when I didn't live here. But adjusting to the small-town atmosphere and avoiding certain people has taken more energy than I imagined. Still, I don't regret moving back home.

I stare at my blue house in the cul-de-sac neighborhood we moved to. The vertical siding gives it a contemporary feel, and the white trim makes my heart happy. It's probably time to break out the Christmas décor since Thanksgiving is next week. I always decorate the outside the day before Turkey Day, yet the thought now feels overwhelming. *A task for future Regina to worry about.*

Shuffling up the sidewalk, I reach for my keys to unlock the door. As soon as I cross into the foyer, my shoes come off, and I sigh in relief. My slippers are waiting on the shoe rack, so I put them on and place my work shoes in their place.

As I stand, an uneasy feeling hits me. Something is off.

"Kyleigh?" I call. Why is it so quiet in here? Usually my daughter has music blasting or some YouTube video up way too loud. It's like she has no concept of volume.

"Where are you, Kyleigh Bear?"

Footfalls greet my ears, and a smile readies my lips. Only it quickly slips off my face when a child who is *not* my own grins at me.

"Hi, Mrs. Parker! Did you have a good day?" She holds up a plate of sugar cookies. "I thought you might like a snack. Kyleigh says you always have one when you get home before you eat dinner."

W-w-what? I have so many questions rattling around in my brain amid the shock. The first being, What is Theodore Evers's daughter doing in my home? Holly is small enough that I know exactly whose child this is.

"Where's Kyleigh?"

"She's at my house, probably offering my dad a snack too."

Did she *make* those cookies in my house? *She's only ten!* A steady pulse begins beating at my temples. "She's not here?" The desire to walk in every single room calling out my daughter's name wells within me. Did my child really go over to some stranger's house?

Okay, so Theodore Evers isn't exactly a stranger, but my daughter doesn't know him, thus making him a stranger. It doesn't matter that *I* know him. Or *how* I know him.

Used to. It's been seventeen years since Theo and I were in each other's orbit. A lot has happened since then. I'm not the girl he used to know, and I'm certain he's not the teenage boy I once adored. There's a reason I'm sneaking around this town instead of sashaying openly down Main Street. You never know where he or his daughter could be lurking, though many of the townsfolk are all too comfortable giving me an update on his life *and* whereabouts.

Amazing how fast these thoughts fly through my mind.

"No, ma'am." Theo's daughter bites her lip as if thinking, then her face brightens. "Should we have some cocoa? I could make it, though Kyleigh says you make the best."

I rub the spot between my forehead that tells me the liquid nectar isn't going to fix any of my problems now. "I think it would be best if we call your father." Only my phone rings before I can say anything else.

One guess who's calling. A glance at caller ID reveals a number I used to know by heart. I swallow down my nerves and answer. "Your daughter is safe."

A sigh greets my ears. "I'm on my way with yours right now."

"Thank you." Before I can tell him where I'm now living, a click resounds in my eardrum.

Guess the Holly grapevine already told him. And judging by the terseness in his voice, Theo is as irritated as I am. Yet I can't bring myself to scold his daughter despite the urge to ask her what in the world she was thinking. What was my own child thinking?

Did they really believe Theo and I wouldn't flip our lids?

I'm barely at a simmer so no telling when the steam will have my lid boiling off.

"Are you mad, Mrs. Parker? Please don't be mad. I don't have a mom around, and I just wanted to know what it's like." Malea's bottom lip pokes out, chin practically touching her chest as her head hangs low.

Oof. Talk about a sucker punch. The yearning in her voice and contrite posture quickly softens my heart. Maybe we should have some hot cocoa after all.

I walk toward the young girl and kneel in front of her.

"What you two did is not okay." I hold in a sigh. "But I'm not mad."

Her head raises so quickly *I* almost get whiplash. "Really? You mean it?"

"I do."

She grins and sticks out her hand. "I'm Malea Evers. It's officially nice to meet you."

"Regina. It's nice to meet you too." Against my better judgment, we shake hands.

I rise to my feet and check my watch. I'm not sure how much farther her dad has to drive since he's coming from his tree farm. *Guess he knew what he wanted all along.* Regardless, I probably have enough time to make some homemade hot cocoa and spend some time with my daughter's best friend.

"Want some hot cocoa?"

"Yes!" Malea makes a fist and pulls it close to her chest with a wide grin.

Just like that, my gut twists. Her smile reminds me exactly of Theo and how much I used to adore that look on his face. Shaking away the memory, I head for the kitchen.

"Kyleigh says you make it from scratch," Malea chatters.

"As close to scratch as possible." I grab some chocolate, vanilla extract (yes, the homemade kind), and other ingredients.

Malea climbs onto the bar stool in front of the island, and I'm reminded that she just has Theo to come home to. I'm not sure how long he's been divorced, but I think someone mentioned five or seven years. But that's not what matters now. If Malea's desperate enough to have a mom that she purposely got off on the wrong bus stop, then I can give her a little idea of how I treat Kyleigh.

"Did you have a good day at school?"

She groans. "They made us read."

"You don't like to read?" Kyleigh has a whole library in her room. *So do you.*

Malea shakes her head fast. "It's boring."

"Have you tried *The Baby-Sitters Club*?"

"What's that?"

I grab my heart and let out a gasp, then shuffle backward in fake shock. Her giggles fill the kitchen, and the sound automatically pulls a small chuckle from me.

"Is that what Kyleigh reads all the time?"

I nod. "Among others. You can go look in her room." I point down the hall. "Last room on the right."

"Okay."

The moment she discovers the treasure trove of books, a loud "Wow" fills the air. Then Malea is running back to the front.

"Don't run," I say automatically.

She grins like she's happy to hear my parental caution. Guess she really is starved for feminine companionship.

You should have her over for a sleepover.

My mouth dries. I *could* invite her over, but that would

mean I'd have to deal with her father. I really, *really* want to continue to avoid that. Remembering the hurt of the past is why I've ducked in stores or hidden around endcaps at the grocery store. I'm not interested in reconnecting with the boy who broke my heart.

As if mocking my hopes and dreams, the doorbell rings, and my stomach drops to my toes. My time of avoiding Theo Evers is over.

Theo

My foot taps impatiently as I wait for Regina to open her door. I peer down at her daughter. Kyleigh looks the same as my ex-girlfriend from the nose down, and every time she stares at me, the color of her eyes startles me. They're the exact shade as Regina's, even if the shape of Kyleigh's eyes probably belongs to her father.

"I'm sure she'll answer any minute," I say to Kyleigh. Though I'm not sure if I'm reassuring her or myself.

She nods just as the sound of a lock reaches my ears. I still myself for the impact that has always been Regina Childs. *Wait, it's Parker now.*

The door swings open, and my breath gets trapped in my chest. How has this woman barely aged? There's still a youthful glow in her honey-brown skin, though her eyes show a weariness that matches the one I imagine is in my own gaze. Life hasn't been kind to either one of us.

"Theo."

I swallow. "Regina."

"Mom!" Kyleigh wraps her arms around her mother, then squeals when she spies Malea.

I arch a brow at my daughter, who slowly walks toward the door. From the way she can barely meet my gaze, she *knows* she's in trouble. Honestly though, I have no idea how I'm supposed to discipline her over purposely getting off at the wrong bus stop.

"Hey, Dad," she mumbles.

"Why don't you come in?" Regina steps back and motions me forward.

Guess it's better to enter the lion's den so the neighbors don't get a reality TV episode in the cul-de-sac.

The house smells like hot chocolate, and the scent is comforting and unnerving all at once. How am I in my ex-girlfriend's house? Ever since she moved back to Holly, I've been aware of her presence. I've made an effort not to cross into her space, remembering all too well our explosive breakup. Words were exchanged that I'm sure can't be forgiven. I was needlessly cruel toward Regina, and the pain her decision caused felt like it crushed my soul. But that was no excuse for how I responded, and hurting her has been one of my biggest regrets. Although I know I played a hand in our breakup, I can't forget the words she flung at me either. How something so good turned so wrong so quickly still baffles me.

I stuff my hands into my pockets as the tension between us rises.

"Would you like something to drink? We made hot cocoa," Regina offers.

"Isn't it the best?" Kyleigh heads right to a kitchen island and sits on a bar stool.

The light blue cabinetry stands out against the white countertops and white backsplash in the kitchen. It's exactly the type of space I can picture Regina cooking in. Blue has always been her favorite color.

Malea glances at me as if asking permission to enjoy some hot chocolate, but judging by the filled mugs, she's already started the drink. Still, I dip my head in acknowledgment, and she takes the seat next to Kyleigh. Regina shuffles a step closer to me, arms folded across her chest.

I rub the back of my neck. "They're crazy, right?"

"Definitely." She squeezes her eyes shut, then opens them. "I'm sorry. I can't imagine the panic you felt."

"Likewise."

She glances at our kids before her gaze flits to mine. "So what do we do about them?"

"I don't know." I could suggest we let the kids hang out, but honestly, I'm not sure I can handle being around Regina that much. I already feel like I need to come out of my skin. But there's also part of me that has so many questions.

Why are you back? Did leaving make you happy? Are you still singing?

Regina looks over her shoulder at the girls, who are whispering and giggling. Honestly, part of me is glad to see Malea so happy. She's stuck with me and doesn't have any womanly influence. But right now, she looks like all is right in the world.

"We can't reward their behavior, right?" Regina whispers.

As if Malea feels my stare, she meets my gaze. A mischievous look sparks in her eyes, and a jolt of fear runs through me. *Nope, do* not *reward her behavior.*

I fold my arms and turn to Regina. "I think we should continue as is. You don't want them to hang out any more than I do."

"What do you know about what I want?" Regina's chin juts out. "You can't read minds, Theodore Evers."

The way my name escapes her gritted teeth makes me

smirk, and the infuriated look that flashes in her brown eyes as a result has me grinning. Is it petty to want to get under her skin as much as she gets under mine? Probably. Will that stop me? Probably not.

"I think I can, Regina. Why else have you refused to let the girls get together after school? Probably because you've been avoiding me."

"Puh-lease. I'm a grown woman. I don't need to avoid anyone."

"Oh really? You've been back in Holly for what, five months, and we haven't run into each other at all?" I purposely exaggerate the time.

Unfortunately, I know exactly when Regina showed up in Holly. Denise, the teller at the local bank, informed me. She remembered we dated and was all too happy to mention my high school girlfriend showing up with a child. Granted the grapevine also informed me when she had married and when she lost her husband, so news of her daughter wasn't a shocker. However, her moving permanently back to Holly might have made me choke on my piece of gum.

Regina narrows her eyes. "Three months."

"And we've *never* run into each other?"

She straightens and meets my pointed stare head on. "Seems like someone has a lot of information. Maybe the truth is *you've* been avoiding *me.*" She points her finger into the center of my chest.

The spark that ignites is nothing but irritation, or so I tell myself. "I'm a grown man. I don't need to avoid anyone." Why I feel so smug throwing her words back in her face is beyond me.

"Ha! You're about as mature as Ms. Brooks."

Ouch. Ms. Brooks should have the title of town crier.

That woman will spread a rumor in a hot second without waiting to see if it's actual truth.

"Fine. If you're mature and I'm mature, then the girls can hang out." I display my hands as if presenting an offer . . . one I'll know she'll refuse, which is exactly what I'm banking on.

She snorts. "I don't know if I can trust my kid in your house."

"Low blow. You know I'd watch over her as if she were my own."

"Likewise. Hence the reason I made my famous hot cocoa for *your* daughter."

I rub a hand across my chin. This woman is so frustrating. Our conversation is just going around in circles. Do we or don't we let the girls hang out? Can I handle seeing Regina Parker that often?

"Um, Mom?"

Regina turns at the sound of Kyleigh's voice. She's staring at her mother with the guilty expression every kid perfects from their toddler stage. Eyes downcast, fingers fidgeting with the hem of her shirt, and exchanging guilty expressions with my child. Malea's look is a little less contrived but no less guilty.

I step forward. "What did you do?"

"Why are you assuming they did something?" Regina interjects.

"Look at them!" I point. I know guilt when it's staring me in the face. Times two.

"Mom, Mr. Evers is right."

Regina's mouth drops, then clamps shut. "Kyleigh Ann Parker, what did you do?" Her voice goes up at the end, dread filling her tone.

"We might have signed you up to help with the Christmas concert."

They did what? Malea grimaces, but I can see the truth of what Kyleigh said in my own daughter's expression. They bamboozled us. They're purposely throwing us together. But to what end?

There's a ringing in my ears, but I fight to stay present because I need to know exactly how many years my child will be grounded. Switching bus stops and signing us up for the Christmas concert when Christmas is my busiest time of the year? Oh yeah, she might get a life sentence.

"Surprise!"

Chapter *two*

Theo

"Malea, what on earth were you thinking?" The words fall from my mouth as soon as we get in my truck. I turn toward my only child. Sometimes she looks like my ex-wife, but right now, the remorseful expression on her face emphasizes a lot of my features. At least they're prettier on her.

"Kyleigh is always talking about her mom and the cool things they do. And I—" She glances away. "I just wanted to know what it's like to have a mom who loves you," she whispers.

My heart shatters at the pronouncement.

I love my child with every breath in me, and I've done all I can to ensure she knows that. Unfortunately, none of that gets rid of the damage her mother did when she walked away from us. I reach over and pull Malea into a hug. She squeezes me tightly, and my shirt dampens from her tears.

My own eyes water up, but I need to be strong for her. There's no crying in fatherhood.

After a few minutes, Malea pulls away. "Are you mad about the Christmas concert?" she asks softly.

I was, but how can I be after hearing how Jianna's absence has affected her? "Not mad, but very frustrated." No, *extremely* frustrated.

The tree farm officially opens next week, but we have a soft opening this weekend for those who have been repeat customers for years. We always hold a raffle and pick thirty people to come to our opening. Everything has to be perfect for tomorrow, and I don't have the time nor brainpower to help the Christmas concert be a success. I had to do some shuffling around just to ensure I could simply attend it. How am I supposed to add twice-a-week practices to my packed schedule?

Malea clasps her hands beneath her chin. "You'll have fun, I promise. We're really good, but Mr. McCall broke his hand when he fell off the ladder putting up Christmas lights. So they need a pianist, and you play so beautifully." She sighs like *Come on.*

And she's right. I can play the piano, though *beautifully* is not a word in my vocabulary. Being in choir means the world to Malea, but I really don't see how I'll have the time to be pianist to her alto. Wanting to put off a no, I end the conversation.

"We'll talk about this later."

We have dinner to get through before I need to be out helping my employees get ready for tomorrow's event. The silence on the drive home is awful, and I want to break it, but what more is there to say? The quiet continues over dinner, and Malea cleans the dishes without prompting.

It's apparent she knows how unhappy I am with the situation, but do I need to make our lives miserable by yapping about it?

I grab a ball cap hanging by the back door and slap it on my head. Maybe chopping some wood will relieve my frustration. I head to the clearing with a stack of wood waiting to be split. This area became the spot anyone on the property could find me after Jianna left without a backward glance. She wanted to pursue a music career in Nashville, so she ended our marriage and gave me full custody. A perverse part of me is happy knowing her name still hasn't hit the billboard charts.

My friend RJ calls this my thinking circle, and he's not wrong. There's something soothing about the rhythmic motions of chopping wood. Lift ax. Swing. Split. Repeat. Even the sound of wood cracking lifts my mood as my thoughts tumble out in a prayer.

I honestly have no idea what I'm supposed to do about Malea, Regina, or the Christmas concert. Where do I find the time? Do I discipline Malea for the stunt she pulled with Kyleigh? If so, how? Next week is Thanksgiving break, and she'll be with me the entire time. Do I just go old-school and remove every single thing from her room except the bed? Or do I choose something simple like taking away screen time?

Why does parenting have to be this challenging?

"Bro, I think you have enough wood."

I let out a huff and rest the ax blade in the stump before turning toward my friend.

RJ stares at me in amusement and juts out his chin, pointing to the chopped wood surrounding me. "Want to talk about it?"

"Not really."

"That's a pretty big pile. You'll supply every employee with firewood if you keep that up."

I scoff.

"Theo, my man, talk to me."

I wipe the sweat from my forehead, then before I realize it, I'm halfway through the story, explaining how I came to knock at Regina Parker's door with her daughter.

RJ lets out a low whistle. "*Regina* Regina?"

I nod.

"Been a minute since I've heard that name. I mean, I knew she moved back, but still . . ."

"Yeah." I hate the way my insides are all twisted. It's like finding that string of Christmas lights from three Christmases ago only to discover they're completely tangled with no hope of straightening the mess out. So you go to the nearest store and buy a whole new set of lights and dump the monstrosity that's been in the attic into the dumpster. Problem solved. Only, I can't take this lump of feelings and trash them.

"How did it feel seeing her?" RJ asks cautiously.

I gesture at all the lumber.

"That bad, huh?"

"Yep."

"That's all you're going to say?"

"Nope." My lips pop against the *p*. My thoughts are still trying to sort themselves out. My hand itches to grab the ax and take a few more swings. I run a hand down my face. "Malea and Kyleigh signed us up to help with the school Christmas concert."

My friend is silent for a moment, then doubles over in laughter. I stare, completely unamused. Finally, RJ wipes tears from his eyes and shakes his head.

"Oh boy. You. Are. In. Trou-ble," he huffs between breaths. He slaps his knee and lets out a last guffaw.

I scowl. "No, Malea should be in trouble."

"Ha, that girl is gonna sleep good tonight. She's probably the one who came up with the scheme."

"How do you know Kyleigh isn't the one?" Or they could've both planned it out.

"Because Malea is your complete opposite in every way. I don't know Kyleigh, but Regina has never been a schemer. She's much more in your face."

Ugh. He's not wrong, but I hate the idea of Malea cooking up plans about switching bus stops and signing parents up for things they have no capacity to do. Being a single parent is hard enough. Add the fact that I run a business, and it feels like I'm drowning most days.

"She needs to be taught a lesson."

"How? You gonna put her in time-out?" RJ rolls his eyes. "Malea's ten going on thirty. Your time-out days are over. What you should be figuring out is how you'll keep your senses around Regina."

"Please. I'm over her." Easy to do when someone makes plans for the future without consulting you, then vanishes like you weren't even a thought in the wind. "We haven't been a thing in over a decade." I wipe away another drop of sweat. Last thing I need is stinging eyes on top of everything else.

"Sure she's not the one who got away?"

"Got away? I'm the one who told her to go!" My voice echoes in the clearing, and I step back. Heat fills my face, and my fists tighten. Purposely loosening my fingers, I twist the visor on my ball cap backward.

"Look," I state more calmly than I feel. "Regina won't be a problem. *I* broke up with her for a reason."

Unfortunately, I'm the fool who met another woman who left me for the same reason: music. Now my daughter wants me to play piano when I've sworn off all performances?

God, help me.

Regina

I'd been looking forward to coming home after a long day at my candle shop, Scents and Sensibility. After having a shipment of candles get lost and an angry customer coming in to complain about something *she* did, coming home should have been a reward. But, no, I had to discover a child that's not mine and find out my kid signed me up for a Christmas concert I want to stay far, far away from. Music is no longer part of my life, and I'm fine with that.

I can't believe my mom convinced me moving back to Holly would be the best thing for me and Kyleigh, because right now it feels more troublesome than I ever imagined. The headache pulsing behind my eye socket agrees with me.

"I'm sorry for worrying you, Mom."

I squint at my ten-year-old. "But not sorry for switching bus stops?"

Kyleigh bites her lip. "I've never known what it's like to have a dad. All the other kids have these jokes with their fathers. Or they go on hikes with them, or they're talking about the upcoming father-daughter dance. But me." Kyleigh points to her chest, tears welling in her eyes. "I don't have that. I don't even have memories of a dad. Just an old picture."

Arrow straight to the gut.

My breath hitches in my chest at the unfairness of it all. Max was a fantastic husband, but one errand to grab more diapers changed our trajectory forever. I've been a single parent practically all of Kyleigh's life. Putting myself in her shoes is all too real. I too wish her dad could be here for all the momentous events and the little memories that are formed every single day. Only he's not coming back, and there's absolutely nothing I can do to change that.

"But, sweetie, you can't just pick a random stranger to become your dad."

"But he's not a stranger. He's my best friend's dad, which means I sort of know him." She raises her brows as if asking me to follow her messed-up logic.

I place a hand on my hip and stare her down. "Have I taught you nothing about stranger danger? If I haven't met them, I don't care how well you think you know them. And even if I *do* know him, you've never met him before, which means what?"

"Stranger danger," she mutters.

"A little louder for the crowd in the back."

"Stranger danger." She throws her hands up in the air. "But, Mom, he's not a stranger. Malea has so many wonderful things to say about him. He even lives on a tree farm. It's like he's Mr. Christmas."

Mr. Christmas? Yeah, right, and I'm Natasha Richardson.

"Regardless if you think he's harmless, the fact is you didn't have my approval." I hate stating the obvious, but the skull on this child is thick.

Her lip pokes out. Sometimes that girl is ten going on

eighteen, and the other times I swear she just left her toddler years.

"Go to your room," I order.

"But—"

Her mouth snaps shut as I twist my face into the *Don't try me* expression I have to wear on occasions. Usually when my one and only child tries every last one of the nerves I possess. Today they're beyond fried.

Kyleigh sulks past me, and I let out a sigh when I hear her bedroom door close quietly. But the silence doesn't offer a reprieve. Grabbing some pain relief from the medicine cabinet, I chug the pills down with my cold hot cocoa. *Blech.* Tomorrow I'll have to figure out what to do with my child, but tonight will be spent wondering how my luck ran out.

Three months back in Holly and not once have I entered the orbit of Theo Evers. It took some juggling, some dodging into random businesses on Main Street or leaving the library parking lot if I spotted his truck. (How he still owns the same one since high school is beyond me.)

Now, not only have I entertained his child with a warm drink and kind words, but Theo and I exchanged a semi-cordial conversation and have to save the Christmas concert since the choir teacher is clumsier than I am.

No wonder why Christmas elves took a pickax to my skull. I need a dark room, quiet, and a reset button. Tomorrow better be February second and offer me a redo, because if the calendar shows the Saturday before Thanksgiving, I'm going to need a new plan for making it through the holidays.

My cell rings as soon as I make it to my room.

"Hey, Ma," I greet.

"Regina, dear, I know I taught you better manners than that."

"Hello, Mother. How are you?" I roll my eyes. You'd think my mom lived in the nineteenth century the way she acts. Sure, I grew up in the wealthier side of Holly, but we're not American royalty. We're upper middle class at best.

Well, *were.* I'm definitely in the lower end since most of my money goes to my candle shop.

"I'm well, dear. Are you two coming over for Thanksgiving dinner? I need a head count."

Right, because she usually has so many people over. It's always me, Kyleigh, Mom, and my dad. That's all we ever have around the dinner table during the holidays. Even when I didn't live here, I still showed up for Thanksgiving, sneaking in and out of town without anyone being the wiser. Anyone being Theo Evers.

"Yes, we'll be there."

"Fabulous. How's my grandchild?"

Up to no good. Since I want to avoid a double migraine, I'll keep Kyleigh's escapades to myself. If I tell my mother what her only grandchild has been up to, she'll end up lecturing me on my sad parenting skills.

"Happy it's Thanksgiving break."

"I bet. Do come over before Thanksgiving so I can spend time with her."

"I will, Mother."

"Good. See you then." She hangs up without another word.

I lie down on my bed. My limbs feel heavy, and the ache in my chest has expanded to my throat. Soon hot tears slide down my face and hit my ears, making my silent weeping turn into real cries.

I'm not even sure what I'm crying about. Being a widow these past ten years? Seeing my first boyfriend again after what was a horrendous breakup? Because what I thought would be a launch into our future was a slammed door of our past, present, and any possible future.

Then again, maybe it's seeing another child who's missing just as much out of life as my own sweet baby. Yet in the back of my head, I'm thinking of how I have to help young singers find their voice when I long since lost mine.

Whatever the reason—*reasons*—my tears lull me to sleep.

Chapter *three*

Regina

"Say the blessing, Jon," Mother says.

Dad doesn't argue, merely bows his head and blesses our food. Mother outdid herself as is evident by all the platters covering the table. It seems a little ridiculous to have so much food for four people, but cooking is one of Mother's favorite pastimes.

At the "Amen," our heads rise, and we begin to pass the dishes around.

"So, Kyleigh, what do you want for Christmas?" Dad asks.

"I don't know, Grandfather." She shrugs, though the side-eye she's giving me clues me in to her unspoken request.

I spoon some sweet potatoes onto my plate and ignore her look.

"Come on, you must know."

She sighs. "Well, I can't have what I want."

"Which is what?"

"A *father.*"

Humph. She's lucky I woke up on the right side of the bed this morning. The sun shone expertly, and not a cloud was visible in the sky. I'm holding on to that beautiful morning no matter how much Kyleigh wants to try my patience.

Dad laughs, then stops as Mother glares at him. "Uh," he stutters. "How do you propose that? Your mom hasn't dated in . . ." He trails off, a look of confusion wrinkling his brow.

"Really, Dad?"

"What?" He feigns innocence.

He's just as bad as Kyleigh.

"It has been a long time, dear." Mother pats her lip with a cloth napkin. "Surely Max wouldn't have wanted you to be this long without another partner."

"Right?" Kyleigh cries. "She needs someone. *I* need someone. We need to be a real family again."

Mother and Father wear twin expressions of pity. I detest that look. My life is good. I have a wonderful daughter (well, most of the time), supportive parents, and my own business. Not many people can say the same thing. So what if the loneliness creeps in from time to time? I'm no stranger to it as it *has* been there these past ten years. That doesn't mean I'm someone to look down upon as if life dealt me a horrific blow I'm incapable of recovering from.

"Kyleigh, be sure to tell your grandparents how you switched places with Malea, thinking you're living the Black version of *The Parent Trap*," I retort.

"I'd be happy to."

Little snot tells the tale like it was a harrowing experience and not an impulsive decision made by two fifth graders. Lord, but I do love her. Even I can see the creative storyteller that is my daughter.

Dad laughs, throwing his head back. His deep chuckle begs me to join in the laughter. It's still so strange to see him with completely white hair and matching beard. But the same kind eyes twinkle from his brown skin and remind me that he's still Dad. My mom is a little on the reserved side, and it takes her longer to warm up to people, but she always looks for ways to care for others. Sometimes I see my traits in both of them. I'm definitely a mash-up baby, whereas Kyleigh is mostly me.

"Wait?" Mother motions for Kyleigh to pause. "You signed your mother up to help with the Christmas concert?"

"Yep!"

"Oh, Kyleigh, what a wonderful thing to do." Mother claps her hands together as if winning an award. "Your mother has the voice of an angel. Your class will be in for a real treat."

My own parents are siding with my child? What multiverse did I wake up in?

"Mother, she *tricked* us. Theo was just as shocked as I was."

"Theo," Mom gasps.

Dad's eyes widen. "Theo Evers?"

"Why do you guys look like you've seen the ghost of Christmas past?" Kyleigh asks.

"Because we have. Your mom and Theo dated in high school."

"Mom!" The whine coming out of my mouth sounds about the same as the one I hear from Kyleigh at times.

I'm slightly embarrassed to sound like I'm full of teenage angst, but angst is definitely what I feel. It's too soon to talk to my child about my life before her father, especially about Theo Evers. If I had my way, my daughter would believe that my dating life started and ended with Max.

Kyleigh's eyes light with speculation and, dare I say it, a plotter's fire. *Lord, have mercy.*

"Wait until I tell Malea."

"Please don't." It's all I can do to prevent myself from rubbing my temples. This child will put me into an early grave with her current scheming, or at least give me a migraine.

Kyleigh nods with a smile as she stuffs a bite of turkey into her mouth. I wouldn't be surprised if that girl has her fingers crossed behind her back.

Lord, dating Theo is going to come back to bite me, isn't it?

Fortunately, Dad changes the conversation. Still, he and Mom give me little glances here and there as we chow down on the Turkey Day offerings. It's like they're saying, *Our poor baby. When did she become so pathetic? Widowhood has really dimmed her personality.*

If they'd walked a mile in my shoes, they'd be a little salty as well. But I keep my mouth shut and eat all the dressing with giblet gravy I can. By the time we finish our meal, a.k.a. have stuffed ourselves to the gills, Dad has made his way in front of the TV to catch up on football, and Kyleigh's watching some YouTuber on her phone. I go to the kitchen to help with the cleanup. Dad helps Mom with the meal, but she has never appreciated his help with kitchen cleanup.

As I rinse a plate under the faucet stream, Mother comes to stand beside me.

"Are we going to talk about Theo?" she asks.

"I'd rather not."

"Will you be able to hold your temper?"

I mentally roll my eyes. "Of course. I'm not a hotheaded eighteen-year-old anymore. God's matured me."

"Hmm. We'll see."

I want to frown or ask her *What does that mean?* But I hold back. Yes, I had a temper in my teenage years. But, yes, the Lord has grown me in all the best of ways. I'm able to bring any anger and injustice I feel to Him and, with His guidance, work out my feelings so I can handle things more calmly. The sass I have leftover is just part of my personality. Take one guess who that came from?

I glance at my mom. "I do plan on being cordial. Our kids are friends, after all." I'd just like them to maintain their friendship within the boundaries of Holly Elementary. Surely that's not too much to ask.

"Right, right." Mother begins to hum to herself.

If my ears don't deceive me, it's the song "Let's Get Together" from the OG version of *The Parent Trap*. I turn and give her a pointed look, but she ignores me and whistles louder instead.

"It's going to be a long Christmas season," I mutter.

Mother laughs, and I let out a huff, but my lips twitch on their own accord. She always manages to pull a laugh from me, even when I don't actually want to.

My thoughts turn back toward the conundrum my child put me in. Part of me is worried that being around Theo will bring out the worst in me. Once we committed to a relationship, it was a whirlwind. Our feelings had been big in the best of ways, like most stereotypical teenagers. Occasionally we'd argue but never over anything that couldn't be fixed by a little makeup session, a.k.a. kiss and forget. Unfortunately, our breakup had been filled with words I don't want to repeat. Already my walls are rising at the mere memory of what Theo *and* I said.

In my teenage years, I fully believed Theo would be *the one*, but obviously I was wrong. The pain of the past makes my throat ache with unshed tears as my defense system—sarcastic mumbling under my breath—tries to rear its ugly head.

Lord, help me remember all You've taught me. I don't want to go back to my old ways. Theo and I are no more, and we're no longer children. We can work together for our kids' Christmas concert, right? Nothing from the past has to be dredged up. I don't have to remember the hurt in his face when I talked about New York or how he let me go without a backward glance.

Not that my dream did me any good. I haven't sung since Max passed away, and I'm okay with that. I have to be. Life doesn't give you your wishes on a platter. Sometimes it serves up a mean side of disillusionment along with heartache. I'll just have to pray that God intervenes and ensures that disappointment isn't waiting for me once again. That has to be good enough for now, because next week I'll have to come face-to-face with my past and connect it with my present.

Malea

"Hold up! They used to date?" My mouth drops as I push my sandwich away and lean closer as Kyleigh tells me all the amazing news she heard at Thanksgiving.

She nods eagerly. "I know, right?" Her twists hang straight down, and her reindeer earrings peek out through her hair with the movement.

"You think this is why they were acting strange when we were at your house?" They had given next-level suspicious vibes.

But what I really want to know is if Dad has been in love

with Mrs. Parker all this time. Would my life look totally different if she were my mom? Kyleigh would be my sister, and I'd never have to know what it was like for your mom not to choose you.

"Definitely. I thought they were just mad at us, but now . . ." Kyleigh takes a bite of her chicken teriyaki.

Mrs. Parker is a great cook. Kyleigh often takes pity on me and lets me try some of her lunch before I have to stuff down the same dry sandwich Dad's been making since kindergarten. Now that it's Christmas tree season, Dad will be even busier, which means my pleas for a new lunch will go unanswered.

My mind moves away from lunch and back to the plan at hand. Now that I know my dad and Kyleigh's mom used to date, it feels like our plan isn't just operating on hope. I mean, if they dated before, surely there are some kind of feelings leftover that Kyleigh and I can spark between them again. I chew my sandwich while thinking.

"What's that look on your face about?" Kyleigh asks. Her head tilts as she studies me.

"Thinking. We're already going to sign them up for the Christmas activities."

Kyleigh bites her lip. "You think we should still enact the plan? They were pretty upset."

"Of course!" I take in a breath to calm myself. Kyleigh is spooked, and I need to reassure her. "Think about it. They used to like each other, maybe even *loved* each other."

"Oh . . ." Kyleigh says slowly.

"Getting them together over and over will re . . . re . . . rekindle"—Ha! That's the word. I heard it on a TV show once—"their feelings again."

"Is that enough?"

I have no idea. I don't know how adult relationships work. But I did watch that Lindsay Lohan movie for ideas because Dad kept muttering under his breath about *The Parent Trap.* I had no clue what he meant but now I do. Thank goodness for streaming apps. Which reminds me . . .

"They used to date!" I hold up my finger in an *Aha!*

Kyleigh frowns. "I said that already. *You* said that already."

"What I mean is, since they dated, we should find out what their very first date was so we can recreate it." That's what they did in the movie. Granted, it didn't work out very well, but in the end they lived happily ever after. That's all that matters, right?

"How are we going to do that?" Kyleigh's nose scrunches up.

"You ask your mom about her first date with my dad. I'll do the same. If that's too difficult, we can always start by asking about our parents and their first date until they share about each other. Whatever information we can gather, we'll share. We'll come up with a plan after that."

Kyleigh nods slowly. "I think I can do that. I don't ask about my dad a lot because my mom always looks so sad afterward."

"I get it. Dad usually goes chop wood after I ask about my mom." We'll never freeze if he keeps it up. "Did you sign us up for the gingerbread house competition?"

She grins. "Yes. Yesterday. I got a confirmation email. Used my school email."

"Yes!" I rub my hands together. "This is going to be great. It's Saturday, right?"

"At two."

"And practice is today, right?" I ask.

Kyleigh nods.

Our parents won't know what hit them. Before they can blink, they'll be falling in love again in no time. Then they'll get married, Kyleigh will be my sister, and we'll all live happily ever after just like in the movies.

Chapter *four*

Theo

The sign in front of Holly Elementary beckons me, but I don't move from my truck. Somewhere in the tan brick building is my daughter. Normally, the idea of seeing her would bring a smile to my face and ease any daily grievances I may have. Today it's Regina Parker that has me gripping the steering wheel while simultaneously asking Jesus to take the wheel. The tight grip I have is a complete contradiction, but the unknown has me wanting to pop antacids. What if I let Jesus take control and He tells me to stop wasting time and apologize to Regina?

You know you should've done that seventeen years ago.

I do *want* to apologize, but I also don't want to end up with egg all over my face. Self-preservation has me wanting to ignore what my conscience says is the right move so I can avoid a broken heart.

So you are *admitting Regina broke your heart?*

Now I'm reminded why I don't have conversations with myself. Nothing good comes from it. A car pulls up right next to me, and I glance over. Regina's peering into the flip-down mirror while applying lipstick. The gesture heats the back of my neck, and I face forward. If she doesn't know I'm aware of her arrival, maybe she'll walk right in and leave me to panic a little more.

A tapping noise jolts me in my seat, and I turn to see her standing outside of my truck. So, nope, she's not going to ignore me. With a sigh, I turn off the engine and pull the key out of the ignition. She backs up when I open the car door. Maybe if I keep my words minimal, I won't insert my foot and cause an argument.

"Hey, Regina."

She dips her head in acknowledgment.

"Wow," I say without thought. "That's it? No *hi*, *hello*, or any other type of greeting?"

Regina props a hand on her hip. "I'm not the one who has trouble saying good-bye to people," she states.

Oh, she wants to go there? "But you don't have a problem hopping a plane and ending a relationship without further communication."

"Oh no." She wags a finger at me. "*You* broke up with *me.*"

We glare at each other, and I'm reminded of that day and how soul crushing it felt. But I keep my lips shut because I don't want to spill my guts and explain why I broke up with her. Or how awful I felt afterward. How badly I handled knowing she was in New York and I was in Holly.

"Are you going to be cordial in front of the kids?" she grits through her teeth.

"Are you? I'm not the one with the temper." Though,

really, we both kind of have tempers. I just hate that I can still notice how beautiful she looks, even when angry.

"Oh, sure, *I'm* the one with the temper. Do you really think your passive-aggressive comments are something to be proud of?"

Nope, but maybe I miss fighting with her and the way we used to make up. *Gah! This is why RJ warned you about your senses betraying you.* I straighten up. "Look, I know how to use my manners in front of children. Will you?"

Her mouth opens, shuts, and opens once more. She raises her hands like she wants to wring my neck before letting out a frustrated scream.

Not gonna lie, I want to laugh, but that might set her off even more. Eighteen-year-old Regina hated being laughed at. Since I'm not trying to laugh *at* her, I make sure my face looks neutral and wait for her to speak.

"I refuse to let you make me lose my temper."

So shouting at the sky isn't losing her temper? Right. "Okay," I say cautiously.

"We will somehow manage to rehearse with the children without losing our cool."

"Agreed."

Her lips purse. "Temporary truce?"

"Fine."

"Wow, so great talking to you." She whirls around on her heel and stalks toward the entrance once more.

I want to applaud that the argument was short-lived. But my heart feels heavy. Regina is still as vibrant as she used to be, and there's a part of me that's drawn like a moth to a flame. But I refuse to get burned this go-around. I'll keep to my side of Holly and let her keep to her side.

After we've been admitted to the school and given visitor badges, we head toward the choir room.

"Do you know what they're planning on performing?" I ask hesitantly. Regina still has steam coming out of her ears, but I need to know the game plan before we walk in front of the students.

"Sort of. Kyleigh's been singing 'Rudolph' and 'Silent Night,' so I'm assuming those are at least two of the songs."

I nod slowly. "I've heard Malea singing those as well."

"You don't think the concert is only two songs, do you?" She wrinkles her nose in that adorable way that used to have me kissing the tip.

Ugh. You have got to stop thinking about the past. I clear my throat. "That does seem too short. Has the choir teacher called you?"

She shakes her head, and I try not to follow the silky strands. Regina's hair is natural, but she always wears it straight. It's like a thick black curtain that makes me want to run my fingers through it.

No, it doesn't. You don't like her, remember?

Still, my fingers twitch by my side.

"I can pretty much play any Christmas song on the piano." It's how I used to relax at the end of the day before Jianna left me. Malea would join me and sing along. Now she's the only person who tries to use the piano.

"Good to know." She bites her lip and glances at me before looking away. "I'm glad you still play."

Not what I said. "Surprised a Christmas tree farmer can do something so talented?" The words are bitter on my lips and hint at the argument that led to our breakup.

"I shouldn't have implied that you would waste your talent if you didn't go to New York." She swallows. "I'm sorry, Theo."

Before I can process the words or the contrition in her eyes, the choir room door opens, and the teacher walks out. His arm is in a neon-green cast and resting in a sling, and he looks miserable.

"Oh, good, you're here. I'm Tim McCall." He holds out his left hand. "Sorry for bad manners, but I can't offer the good hand." He looks tired and barely awake but happy just the same.

"Are you okay?" Regina points to his cast. "Shouldn't you be home?"

"My wife is going to smother me if I stay in that place one more minute." His eyes are wide, and he runs a hand through his hair, making it stand on end. He's got the nutty professor vibe going for him—Jerry Lewis version.

Regina chuckles. "We just like to take care of our men."

I have to keep the shock off my face. Who is she, and where's the woman who vowed she'd take care of no man when we were together? First she's apologizing, now she's sounding like taking care of a man is the greatest thing ever.

She did lose her husband.

Ugh, I'm a jerk. I can't imagine what it's like to lose your spouse when you envisioned a lifetime with them. Sure, Jianna left me high and dry, but she's alive. One day she may decide she wants a relationship with Malea, and our daughter will have the chance to repair what's been broken. But Kyleigh will never see her dad again. That perspective brings Regina's actions to a whole new light.

Lord, please ease their pain.

Maybe losing a spouse forever is what changed Regina. It makes her offer of a temporary truce more palatable. The least I can do is make it through the holidays being cordial. It doesn't mean I have to let down the wall that's guarding my heart. My heart does *not* need to grow three times its size.

Regina

We are not going to make it through this rehearsal. Since when did ten- and eleven-year-olds get so grown? Theo and I have their rapt attention as they wait for us to answer the girl in front—I think she said her name was Crystal—who asked if we were dating.

"Actually, our personal lives are really none of your business."

I throw a glare at Theo. If that's not waving a red flag in front of these kids, I don't know what is.

I step forward. "How about we focus on the concert?" I stare at everyone, giving my best stern-mom look. A few kids straighten up, especially Kyleigh and Malea. "Mr. McCall will be in his office if we need assistance, but Theo and I have been involved in music since we were children."

True, but let's ignore how long of a hiatus I've taken from the craft I used to love. The kids nod and watch me expectantly. My throat feels dry, and I wish there was a glass of water I could drown my nerves with. Instead, I think of the list of songs Mr. McCall said he wanted the class to sing.

"Let's start with 'Rudolph.'" I pick up the baton and hold it in the air.

The kids rearrange themselves on the risers as Theo goes to the piano. At his nod, I raise my hands and say, "From the top," then begin conducting.

At the sound of the children's voices, I hold in my surprise because they're good. They're *really* good. Guess I thought fifth-grade choir wouldn't impress me, sort of like hearing the fifth-grade band put on a concert after having just a semester to learn an instrument. But the sound of their sweet voices captivates my heart.

I expect to hear some off-key moments, which of course there is a kid or two off tune. However, there's an infectious innocence to their tone that makes me smile and feel the magic of Christmas. You know that kindness that pervades every person's actions and makes you wish that people could be this nice all year round? Or the wonder of all the Christmas lights and the enchanted vibe they give off when you're walking down Main Street at night in Holly? Every storefront decorates for the Christmas season, adding to the joy. That wonderment is what the kids' singing evokes in me. If I have to blink rapidly to keep all the liquid from pouring out of my eyes, then so be it.

After they finish, I clap my hands, as does Theo.

"I don't think you guys need me up here."

"We do, Mom!" Kyleigh shouts from the alto section.

I laugh. "We'll see. Let's hear 'Silent Night,' okay?"

The kids nod, and we run through the song once. This one's a little rougher, which means we'll definitely need to break out and work on those patches. Theo prefers to express his musical talent on the keys, but his voice is just as magical as hot cocoa with peppermint. I don't have to acknowledge that out loud in order to have him work with the tenor and bass singers.

I break us into two groups, taking the altos and sopranos. The girls gather close to me as we go over one of the parts that needs finessing. There's a knot growing in my throat as the music swirls around me, calls to me. In order to help these kids, I'm going to have to sing out loud at some point.

But the person in me who's been hammered by life and flattened by trial after trial would rather coach them without my vocal cords working in tandem with them.

When the children take their places on the risers once more, "Silent Night" is a lot more cohesive and has me tearing up once again. I need a break. I turn to Theo, who looks just as discombobulated as I feel. "Give me a moment while I get the other music from Mr. McCall."

I head behind one of the curtains, where the choir teacher stated his office was located. As I enter the room, I'm taken aback by the papers strewn all about. Old sports drink bottles fill the trash can (at least there's that), and there's not a single thing in order. The place resembles a teenage boy's room. Would the teacher claim he knows where everything is if I were to ask?

"Hey, Mrs. Parker. Everything okay?" he asks.

"Do you have the music sheets for the other two songs?" I ask.

"I do." He riffles through a pile to the right and hands over a purple folder that has "Christmas Time Is Here" and "Winter Wonderland" inside.

"Thank you so much."

I hand Theo the piano pieces, then pass out the students' sheets to the class. After informing the students of the two new songs we're going to learn, we launch into an attempt at "Christmas Time Is Here." The rest of the rehearsal is spent teaching them the piece, which means I end up singing as an example.

The first note that clears the air has my face heating. The impact of Theo's stare has the memories roaring back. Images of us together at his house growing up flash through my mind. Recollections of him playing piano and me singing by his side. The teenaged girl back then was so foolish, thinking her boyfriend would go off to college with her and major in music as well. Somehow my plans for college became *our* plans for college without ever asking Theo his opinion on the whole matter. It wasn't until the day we broke up that I realized I had never verbally asked what he wanted for his future. Unfortunately, I didn't handle our parting well, and every hurt came spilling out in ugly words.

My eyes prick, and I drag in a breath, hoping tears don't make an entrance. Now's not the time to get lost in my thoughts and imagine what would've happened had we both handled our emotions more maturely. Though I've blamed Theo all too often, I have to admit I had the maturity of a mosquito back then.

Are you really any better now? Do you not remember that scene back in the parking lot?

I grimace inwardly. Why I let Theo Evers make me so frustrated continuously baffles me. How can I say I've matured when I go screaming in frustration at the least provocation? Yet, he didn't laugh, and old Theo *definitely* would have.

If he's matured, then I can too.

I push the concept away and get back to rehearsal. By the time we're done, and the kids begin filtering out, I'm exhausted.

I put on my coat and grab my purse. "Kyleigh, you ready?"

"Um, actually . . ." She glances at Malea.

I hate how my Spidey senses kick in and the very real tango my insides start doing. "What now?"

Theo freezes behind me, and the girls come to stand in front of us. They hold each other's hands as if gaining moral support. My stomach knots tighter. *God, prepare me.*

But my body can't brace any tighter than it already is. I'd shatter if I were glass.

"We might have signed all of us up for the gingerbread competition," Kyleigh says.

"Say what now?" Theo asks.

"It's Saturday at two," Malea adds. "The entrance fee was twenty dollars."

"Twenty dollars?" Theo and I say simultaneously.

We glance at each other, then back at the girls.

"Where did you get twenty dollars from?" Theo asks.

"Our allowance."

He pinches the bridge of his nose. "Then get it back. We're not doing that."

Malea stares at Kyleigh, then speaks. "It's nonrefundable."

I groan. I would never have thought it possible, but now I know the truth. These girls are going to kill us with togetherness. What a Christmas tragedy.

Chapter *five*

Regina

What does one wear to a gingerbread competition with their ex-high school boyfriend in attendance? Am I supposed to look cozy cute and wear a sweater that makes me look huggable to make him regret ever breaking up with me? Or am I supposed to look like the thirty-plus-year-old mom to a ten-year-old girl that I am? Oh yeah, and my daughter's BFF will be in attendance, which means we'll probably look like a legit family to the untrained eye.

Who knows what the town gossips will believe about our little outing.

Knowing the girls used their allowance quickly changed the dynamic, and soon Theo and I were kowtowing to our kids' shenanigans once more. What I really need to figure out is how to put a stop to their schemes.

Lord, please help me out!

A rap of knuckles interrupts my last-ditch effort of a prayer to find Kyleigh standing in my doorway.

"Hey, Kyleigh Bear. What are you up to?"

"I was reading, then realized it's almost time to go." Her eyes widen. "Why are you still in your robe?"

I motion to her cute outfit. "Not everyone can look as adorable as you." She's wearing a long-sleeve reindeer shirt and overalls. I want to squeeze her and tell her to stop growing, but I just barely resist the urge.

"Mom, you're beautiful." A gleam enters her gaze as she steps in front of my closet. She shuffles through my clothes and then yells, "Aha!"

She pulls out an emerald-green mock turtleneck and black jeans. "Just add your nativity earrings for that Christmas vibe."

My fifth grader is dressing me. I'm not sure whether to feel thankful or sad that I'm this desperate. Nevertheless, I dress exactly as she says before staring at my hair. I plug in my flat iron, then add some ringlets and pin some to the top of my head. *Not bad*. Says I tried but not too hard.

Hopefully Theo thinks this is how I leave the house regularly and not that I want his attention.

Do you want his attention?

I shake my head. Had it once and I don't need to return to that path. We're too different, and I'm okay with that. Max fit me better. Our life was calm and steady, just what I needed. And oddly enough, my widowhood has been much of the same, well, after the intense grief settled to an everyday, manageable kind. Now when I think of Max my heart is able to remember him without that wave of grief that was the first few years of overwhelm.

"Mom, come on!" Kyleigh shouts.

I grab my red sling bag and peacoat. "Coming!" *Good grief, someone's impatient.*

"It's a competition. We have to be the best."

My lips lift in amusement. "And if we're not?"

"We will be." Kyleigh grabs my hand, and I give it a squeeze.

I'm so thankful for the little moments when she reminds me of her precious toddler days in the midst of glimpses of her teenage future. Lord knows I'll need to be reminded of how much I love her when we sync up and I'm calling on the Lord's strength not to lose my ever-loving mind.

The heater warms us as we drive from our cozy neighborhood to Main Street, where all the Christmas activities take place during the season. Though it's already dark, the streets are bright with white lights. Every shop's frame and roof are draped with white lights, as well as the light poles and trees sprouting here and there. There's a wreath on almost every storefront and garland strategically draped around columns. I even spy some candy canes hanging from the greenery. Since I was part of beautifying Main Street for the holidays, the décor shouldn't surprise me, but it does. It's like getting a book you preordered or like a Christmas gift you completely forgot was on your wish list.

A sedan leaves a parking space right in front of the bakery hosting the event. Even though parallel parking is one of the seven horrors of this world—the others are getting wet when not in a shower/pool, rain after you just got your hair done and you're without an umbrella, a swallow of orange juice, no coffee when you desperately need a cup, a kid puking in your bed, and running into your ex because your child orchestrated it—I'll attempt my hand to avoid parking far away.

Kyleigh and I walk into Time of Knead, and immediately, Malea waves a hand in the air from a table in the back corner. It's like my gaze locked in of its own accord. To my horror—Ugh, why is that word suddenly a part of my repertoire?—Theo is wearing a green turtleneck. I glance down at my child to ask a question, but she's already weaving around tables to get to her best friend.

I don't want to think she set me up to dress like my high school sweetheart, but what else am I supposed to believe? This whole experience has been a nightmare I can't wake from. My steps feel like I'm trudging uphill, and when I finally get to the table, Malea thrusts an apron my way.

"The aprons came with the registration." She grins, her brown eyes lighting with joy.

She's filled with the holiday spirit, and I'm pretty sure I'm green with a heart two sizes too small. I don't want to wear matching aprons and pretend we're a family. I want to stomp my feet and go whining to my mom. Then again, she seems to be rooting for Kyleigh's evil plans to prevail, so maybe not the appropriate person to have a pity party with.

Guess You're stuck listening to me whine, Lord. Why, oh why, do I have to match Theo? Why do we have to look like we belong to each other right now? It's too much.

Because teenage me would've loved every moment of this. I would've snapped a selfie and made it my phone wallpaper. Teenage me had such forever plans with Theodore Evers that today me wants to hit old me with a brick like Kevin did to Marv in *Home Alone 2: Lost in New York.*

I mentally brace myself, then hang my peacoat on the hook along with my sling bag before donning the apron. As I tie it behind my back, I see the little snowman all over the red garb. Okay, so the apron is actually adorable. Kyleigh will probably be breaking these out as we bake over the holiday. It's tradition to make sugar cookies and cinnamon rolls for the season.

"Listen up, everyone!"

I turn at the sound of the bakery owner's voice. "I'm going to go over the rules of the competition," Lillian states. "You have thirty minutes to make your gingerbread creation. You'll be judged on creativity, structure, and holiday spirit." She counts each attribute off on her fingers.

The girls whisper excitedly, and my Grinch heart thaws—Grows?—a little bit at the happiness on their faces. But when I lock eyes with Theo, I whirl back around to face Lillian. I do *not* need to have a moment with him.

"All materials have been provided, as you can see at your table. However, if you need more of the adornments, like gumdrops or peppermints, please come see me, and I'll get you what you need. Any questions?"

Shakes of the head and a chorus of no's ring out around the room. Looks like the people of Holly are ready to compete for the best creation.

"Great, then the time begins now."

Kyleigh, Malea, Theo, and I all lean forward around our table. My gaze catches Theo's, and it's all I can do to maintain a neutral expression. The mere sight of him makes me aggravated. Why did he have to dump me all those years ago? Why couldn't we have come to some kind of compromise?

Probably because you said his talent would waste away and his dreams would suffocate a slow death in Holly. I mentally wince. Yep, yep, I said those things, and I hate that I let heartache turn me petty. I don't want to feel awkward like this around him. Even though I apologized at the school, there's still a sense of unease between us. Do we have more to say to each other?

"What's the plan?" Theo asks, looking back and forth at our girls.

"What if we make one of our homes?" Malea asks.

"Maybe, but shouldn't we do something totally Christmasy?" Kyleigh asks.

"The bakery?" Theo says. "Like it's decorated for the season?"

"That's an idea, or we could do Main Street," I suggest with a shrug. All of the ideas sound good.

"Oh, Main Street." Malea's eyes get all big. "That one."

She's so sweet that I accidentally share a smile with Theo. I correct myself and stare at my child, who nods with a grin.

"Let's do it." Kyleigh claps her hands together.

We discuss a plan for the next few seconds. Once we have a strategy in place, we start erecting a storefront façade for some of the businesses on Main Street, using icing to differentiate between the bakery, my candle shop, and the local salon.

"How about we add the coffee shop as well?" Theo asks.

"Four looks better, so yes."

"Mark this day down. Regina Parker agrees with me." Theo makes a show out of pulling his phone up and notating in his calendar app.

My eyes narrow, but the smirk on his face doesn't lift. I *hate* that he looks good with that expression on his full lips. His milk chocolate skin is blemish free, and his goatee looks like it's been treated with beard oil. Though the hair lining his jaw isn't in full beard pattern, it still looks good.

He's stupid good looking.

Stop looking at him.

As if he can hear my thoughts, Theo's smirk turns into a full-fledged grin. I avert my gaze and pick up the icing. Time to continue decorating and ignore the fluttering of my pulse. Thank goodness my hairstyle falls to my shoulders so he can't see the erratic pulse pounding in my neck. Why, oh why, does Theo Evers have to make me feel this way?

Thirty-plus-year-olds shouldn't react to men this way, Lord. I certainly didn't have this hormonal craze with Max. My eyes tear up. How awful does that make me? My pulse may have never pounded over my husband, but my heart remained steady with a glow of love.

You loved Max. Don't let Theo Evers mess with your head.

Theo

If a woman hates your guts, shouldn't that stop you from noticing how appealing she looks? I mean, only Regina can make a simple turtleneck and jeans look like she belongs on a cover of a magazine. And let's not discuss how we're wearing the same shade of green. If I hadn't picked out the shirt myself, I would've thought Malea was up to one of her tricks again. As it is, there's no one to blame but myself.

When Regina and I dated before, we often dressed alike but never on purpose. We'd meet up and end up discovering we were wearing the same color. If we weren't so different, I'd marvel at how synced our brains are. But Regina has never had trouble reminding me how different we are.

As we make the gingerbread street with our daughters, I see way too many similarities between new Regina and the one I used to know. The soft way she smiles at Kyleigh. The amusement in her gaze when her daughter tells a joke and the gentle way she keeps her on task.

I always knew Regina would be a fantastic mother, but seeing it in person hits right in the sternum. Seeing the way our daughters interact is also bittersweet. I've always wanted a big family, but Jianna wanted to stop at one child. Said we could lavish all of our attention on Malea. Then she left to chase her dreams in Nashville, leaving me to pick up the pieces. The amount of YouTube videos I've watched on parenting is ridiculous. I spend way too much time on social media looking for parenting tips, especially for men raising young girls.

But they work.

For all intents and purposes, Malea is well adjusted, not including this switcheroo stint. I'm still waking up daily from shock that Regina is back in my life. Not just being able to watch her around town—in a non-stalker/creeper kind of way—but at the rehearsals and now here. There's so much I want to say to her, but words halt in my throat every time I see her.

Her beauty has always rendered me silent. It was always in an *I can't believe she's my girl* kind of way. Now it's more of a *What went wrong?* or *How can I fix this?* Not that I want the fix to lead back to a relationship, more like cool the animosity between us and absolve my guilt. God hasn't answered my questions on how to repair the damage of the past, but I'll keep on asking until I figure out how to not be so awkward around her . . . or antagonistic.

Right now, the silence is killing me, so I do what every dad in America does. Tell a joke. "What do gingerbread men use when they break their legs?"

Malea groans, knowing where this is headed. I regale her with a dad joke at least once a day.

"Dad, please," she mutters.

"What?" Kyleigh smiles at me, all ears.

"Candy canes."

She giggles. "Good one. Do you have another?"

I stare at Malea as if to say *Someone likes my jokes.* My child can make rolling your eyes an Olympic sport, so I turn my focus on Kyleigh.

"What do you call an old snowman?"

"What?" Regina says automatically.

I'm not gonna lie, hearing her engaged does something to me. I gaze into her pretty eyes, wait a beat, and say, "Water."

All the girls laugh at that one, and my lips quirk into a smile. It's not every day a dad joke ends in laughter.

"Do you know any others?" Kyleigh asks.

"Hm. I've got one more. You ready?"

She nods.

"What's every elf's favorite type of music?"

She tilts her head, then shrugs. "I don't know."

"Wrap!" Regina and I say together.

We meet each other's gaze, then fall over laughing. Of course the joke's not that funny, but the look on her face at having guessed correctly is enough to tickle my funny bone.

"I've got a better one," Malea announces.

"Go for it, squirt."

"Dad," she mutters out the side of her mouth.

Regina chuckles, and I have to resist the urge to puff out my chest. What is it about this woman that has me reverting to my high school days?

"Okay. Why do reindeer like Beyoncé so much?"

Kyleigh gasps. "Because she sleighs!"

My mouth drops. "Where did you hear that?"

"I made it up, Dad." She shakes her head like I'm some old man that can't get with the times.

Granted, having a fifth grader who acts more like a teenager every day makes me feel ancient in comparison. I don't understand half the words out of her mouth. Like what is a skibidi? And I'm pretty sure the way she uses sigma isn't in reference to any fraternity. Was my slang that difficult for my own parents to grasp? At least I know one term. Probably because I think half the words out of her mouth are brain rot. (See what I did there?)

The girls are putting on finishing touches of gumdrops when a bell chimes in the room. All talking ceases as we naturally shift our gaze toward the center of the store.

Lillian steps onto a chair and cups her mouth. "Time's up. Please have one person bring your creation to the front for the judging ceremony."

The ladies all point to me, and I grin.

"Good thing you brought the muscle." I wink. And maybe my gaze is purposely directed at Regina.

"Well, we certainly didn't bring the brain." She tosses a sly smile my direction.

Ouch. Instead of acting wounded, I lean close. "Oh, I'm both brain *and* brawn."

There's a little catch in her breath that brings a satisfied smile to my face. Instead of staring at her once more, I gather our creation on the cardboard they provided and slide my hands underneath. My steps are slow until I set the multi-storefront down on the table for judging. Lillian places a number in front of our gingerbread creation and hands me a copy of that number.

When I return to the table, Regina averts her gaze, avoiding my stare, which tells me I'm flustering her. Literally, all I could ever want in life. If Regina Parker is flustered by me, I'm doing something right.

"While our judges have a moment examining all the creations, please help yourself to some milk and cookies."

"Yes!" Malea does a dance, and we all laugh.

"Want to grab some with me?" I ask Regina. "I'll probably need the help."

She nods. I say nothing as we walk to the refreshment table, but then the pressure gets to me and a question erupts.

"How'd you start the candle shop?" I stuff my hands in my pockets. *That's the best you can do?*

"Oh." She blinks. "Well, it started as an Etsy shop and me working at home when Kyleigh was a baby. Then when Max passed away, I lived with a friend for a while. Her husband had divorced her and left her with a huge house. She didn't have any kids, which meant the house was way too big for her. So I saved money and made candles."

"Did you live with her the whole time?"

Regina shakes her head. "No. Just for a year, but I lived close by."

"And you moved back to Holly this summer to open your own shop?"

"Pretty much. Mom told me when the store came up for sale. I prayed about it and felt like God was calling me home."

"That's great. I'm happy for you." *Do it. Say it.* "And I'm, um, I'm sorry. Sorry for what I said and how I left things." I meet her gaze so that way she can know I'm sincere. "It's my biggest regret."

She studies me and then slowly nods. "I'm sorry too, Theo."

A weight lifts off me, but wariness fills the space. Because if I'm forgiven and forgive Regina, what's to prevent my heart from tumbling at her feet once again?

Chapter *six*

Theo

We won.

The kids are on cloud nine and talking a mile a minute. Great, I'm thinking in clichés because my brain is operating at low power. The time with Regina has me too reflective, and all I want to do is retreat to my house and go chop some wood.

Instead, I watch as the girls exclaim over their blue ribbon and discuss how they're going to spend their gift card for the bakery.

"How about an after-school snack?" Kyleigh suggests.

"Ohh." Malea turns to me. "Can we do it Monday?"

I grimace. "Sorry, squirt. Monday we have rehearsals."

"Then an after-rehearsal snack," Kyleigh exclaims.

Regina and I exchange glances. I don't like how instinctive it is. Even more, I hate that I can read her mind. She wants to let the girls down easy and part ways. We've let our children hang out, now we should stop. That line of thinking shouldn't bother me because I literally just had the same thought. However, Regina wanting a way of escape is too reminiscent of our past.

"Sweetie, why don't you let Malea have the card. We'll go to the bakery a different time."

Kyleigh's brow furrows. "Why wouldn't I share it with my best friend, Mom? It's not like it's too far for us to drive."

"No, but Malea and Mr. Evers don't live in town."

Great. She *Mr. Evers*'d me. "It'll be fine. We can plan a time for the girls to meet up." I meet Regina's gaze with a nonchalant air as if I'm unbothered by the idea. Apparently, Petty is my middle name.

It's like my heart wants to protect itself on instinct, but when Regina tries to react in the same way it gets under my skin. She's the one who wanted a different life, and now she's here in Holly, though she once claimed the town was too small for her and her dreams. Never mind that *I* was in Holly. She shouldn't be the one trying to avoid me. I should be the one avoiding her, and the heartache that comes with knowing I'm not good enough.

Then let them go to the bakery on their own, and you take Malea and use the gift card.

"Fine. We'll set up a time later." Regina hikes her purse strap over her shoulder and clings to it. "Kyleigh, how about we head home now?"

Her daughter exchanges glances with mine, and my stomach drops to my toes. Instead of looking upset that they have to part, they each look like they're urging the other to speak. *Oh boy.* That means they have more in store. I know it as well as I know Regina and I will both need to temper our reactions.

"Now what?" My tone is resigned and wary.

Regina's eyes widen, and she stares at her daughter.

"Well . . ." Kyleigh starts.

"We've been having so much fun together," Malea adds.

"So we thought we should keep the merriment going." Kyleigh smiles bright at the proclamation as if hoping her mother and I will agree.

Too bad that smile is faker than all those social media filters. I fold my arms and widen my stance, physically bracing for the impact of their next words.

"Really, girls? What now?" Regina asks.

"Next Saturday is the snow-family competition," Malea states.

My head falls back as my gaze looks heavenward. *Help me*. The snow-family competition? How did I go to sleep and wake up in a maze I can't get out of? Each day is repeating with time alone with Regina and Kyleigh. Somehow I keep making wrong turns because I can't seem to escape the togetherness. Something I would've craved like air when we dated in high school now feels like a trap. How much more can my heart take before it succumbs to the force of nature that is Regina Parker?

"Did it cost money to register?" Regina asks.

"No, but the winner does win money," my daughter says. "It's one hundred dollars. We could split it four ways." She throws me a mischievous look. "I learned that at school."

"Be proud," Kyleigh adds. "She hates math."

Don't I know it. I feel the same way, but I pretend for Malea's sake because she needs the encouragement to bring her grade up.

I squeeze the bridge of my nose, hoping to stay the headache forming.

"We'll discuss this later," Regina states with finality. "Let's go home, Kyleigh."

"Yes, ma'am." Her shoulders droop, and her head drops.

I hate to see her like that, but I understand the self-preservation driving her mother. Without a word, I motion for Malea to follow me. We parked a block away from Main Street, and our walk is completed in silence. Puffs of air escape my mouth as we find my blue truck. Before putting the vehicle in drive, I make sure Malea is buckled, then we're off.

After a few minutes, Malea speaks.

"Dad?"

"Hm?" I drag myself from my thoughts. "What's up?"

"Why did you and Mrs. Parker break up?"

I blink at her. "How did you know we dated?"

"Kyleigh told me."

Did Regina tell her daughter, or did Kyleigh overhear a conversation she shouldn't? Regardless . . .

"It's grown-up stuff. Don't worry about it." But I can tell from the lasers heating my cheek that Malea's not going to give this up. I look at her fully. Yep. She's staring but with curiosity and not condemnation. I face forward once more.

"We wanted different things," I explain. "So we broke up. She left Holly and I stayed." Just like Jianna left and I stayed. Why am I so easy to leave behind?

The thought makes my throat ache, and I grip the wheel.

"Did you love her?"

Why is my child going for the jugular?

"Does it matter?" My words are cold as I try to push against the emotions threatening to overtake me.

"I mean," she says in a small voice. "Maybe this is a chance to start over?"

I squeeze my eyes shut—briefly since I don't want to crash. The timidity of her voice has my heart in a vise grip. I don't want my daughter to hesitate when talking to me, but I very much want to tell her to mind her own business. This is a subject *I'm* having difficulty facing, let alone talking out loud about to my child.

"Squirt, being a grown-up isn't easy, just like being a kid isn't."

I see her nod in my periphery.

"Have you prayed about it? You're always telling me to ask God for help and guidance. Maybe this is one of those times He can help you. Maybe He *wants* you to start over with Mrs. Parker."

Out. Of. The. Mouth. Of. Babes.

"Promise you'll ask Him?"

I don't want to, but when your kid asks you to pray, that's exactly what you do. "I promise."

Regina

Nothing relaxes me more than making candles. I stare in my work cabinet that houses all my essential oils. My Christmas scents are selling fast, which means I need to make more of the popular ones.

Grabbing the cinnamon, nutmeg, and sweet orange essential oils, I set them to the side. The pine needle, myrrh, and peppermint go to the other side. Then I take the white fir, cedar, and vanilla and place them in front of me.

My wax is about melted, so the next step is to add the scents before pouring it into the heated jars. The shop has a small alcove that's like my mad scientist laboratory. Though

I still try out brand-new combinations at home. No use stinking up the shop and scaring customers away.

My cell rings, and I smile at the name on my caller ID.

"Kris! How are you?" I haven't talked to my old housemate/friend in a couple of weeks.

"Questioning my sanity."

My brows raise automatically. "What's going on?"

"I sold my house, most of my possessions, and packed the rest in a trailer. I just pulled over for a bathroom-and-snack break."

Whoa. "Are you on the road?"

"Um, actually, I'm on my way to Holly."

My mouth drops. Kris is *not* the impulsive type, but the thought of seeing her again makes me happy. I haven't seen her since Kyleigh and I moved to Holly.

"What brought this on?"

"I feel stuck, G. Although time continues to march on, I feel like I haven't. My life is the same as it was when you lived with me. I needed to shake things up." She pauses. "Is it okay if I stay with you?"

"Of course you can." She let me move in with a crying baby. The least I can do is offer a room in return.

"Do you think I'm being reckless?"

"I'm assuming you prayed about this?"

"I did."

"Then that's all that matters. If God told you to shake things up, listen." Who am I to judge?

But what about you? Are you listening to Him?

I'm not sure where those questions came from, but that little prick of conviction hits me in the center of my chest. Is there something I'm not doing that I should be?

"Thanks, G. I should get there tomorrow."

I blink, my thoughts shifting to the background. "Okay. I'll have the guest room ready."

"You're the best."

"See you tomorrow."

When the call ends, I let out a sigh. I'm not sure what my friend's really thinking because I know how much Kris loved her house. But if she felt the need to sell it, who am I to question her motives? I made a big move this summer, and I can honestly say it's been great. I still feel a little lonely at times, but being near my parents, watching Kyleigh bloom, it's all been worth it.

My thoughts turn back to the gingerbread competition. After the initial awkwardness, building our creation was actually fun. Malea has the best sense of humor, and she and Kyleigh feed off each other. A blessing and an inconvenience since they're determined to get Theo and me together at every opportunity.

Lord, what do I do about the snow-family competition? I used to love doing it as a kid with my mom and dad. We'd gather items to decorate our snowmen before the competition. Since Holly is in the Sierra Nevada mountains, snow isn't always present. They'll probably have to pipe artificial—made from snow machines—snow in for the competition.

After making ten of the Holiday Simmer candles, I move on to the next fragrance. When I'm done creating all the different scents and pouring the wax into the respective jars, I have ten candles with the Holiday Simmer, Christmas Pine, and Christmas Sweater fragrances.

The rest of the afternoon passes quickly, and I find myself in front of the elementary school way too soon. Theo's truck is already in the parking lot, and I begrudgingly take the spot next to him.

"Regina," I whisper. "You've gotta get yourself together. Theodore Evers is *not* losing any sleep over you so don't give him the satisfaction."

His life seems exactly how he wanted. A Christmas tree farm that's the darling of Holly and a beautiful little girl. The only hiccup is the ex-wife.

Seems like both of your plans had a little detour.

When I told Theo I wanted to go to New York and make it on Broadway, he laughed. Told me we were small-town folk, not city people. When I insisted he could make a life in the city as well, especially since his talent on the piano was evident, he got angry and accused me of messing up our future plans. Turned out our dreams were vastly different. The whole miscommunication-at-its-finest thanks to us being teenagers in love. Who knew you needed to communicate your wants, needs, and desires to avoid catastrophe?

Although we exchanged apologies, I find my insides are still a squirmy mess. The armor I'm used to wearing around him to avoid the pain of the past makes me want to lash out the moment I step out of my vehicle. *You are thirty-five years old. God has worked on your heart. You don't need to revert to a moody teen.* Basically, I need to act like I'm saved.

"Forgive us our trespasses as we forgive those who trespass against us."

I wince at the reminder but make an inward promise to heed it.

Turning off the engine, I gather my things and meet Theo on the sidewalk. "Hey," I say softly.

"Good day so far?" His dark brown eyes search mine as if he really wants to know.

"It's been productive."

"Same." He lets out a long exhale. "Look, I have something to say."

I nod. Why is my mouth dry all of a sudden?

"That day . . . I handled it so badly, G."

Tears prick at my eyelids at the sound of my nickname on his lips. "I didn't do that much better."

"Yeah, but I laughed at your dream instead of telling you how much I believed in you. I should've told you how phenomenal your voice is. How hearing you sing always brings me peace. Instead, all I could see were my plans going up in smoke. It never occurred to me that we could somehow merge our dreams."

Same. All I could feel was panic that Theo wasn't coming with me to New York.

"I'm truly sorry for hurting you," he says.

Why is there a sob trapped in my chest? Can I blink fast enough to keep my eyes dry and my emotions safely inside? This is exactly what I needed to hear, but now I need to be alone to properly grieve the past.

"Thank you," I rasp. It's all I can do to force the words from my throat—raw with unshed tears. Still, there's more I have to say. If he can be sincere, so can I. If he can be honest, then I'll find the nerve to be as well.

"I'm sorry too, Theo. I should've realized how much Holly meant to you. You talked about owning the tree farm so often, but I just pretended like it would happen *after college.* I didn't really listen, and I'm sorry." I take a breath. "Also, I should've told you a lot earlier about New York instead of dropping that grenade at graduation."

I pause to gather the rest of my thoughts. "I think deep down, I knew what your answer would be, and I wanted to prolong our relationship. You've always been honest about wanting to be in Holly."

He stuffs his hands into his jean pockets. It's not fair that he can make flannel look so good. Or that his body has filled out with muscles while mine has softened with age.

"Thank you for saying that."

We stare at each other for a moment.

"Are we good?" he asks cautiously.

I tilt my head, giving his question actual consideration. Because I don't want to walk around Holly trying to avoid my ex any longer. I'm a long way from eighteen and what can be blamed on immaturity shouldn't have such a stronghold on me in my mid-thirties. *Am I good, God? Because I want to forgive him as much as I want to believe he's forgiven me.*

Maybe that's what the Lord has been waiting for me to admit because a supernatural peace comes over me. I don't have to carry this hurt any longer.

"I forgive you, but it might take a moment to be truly good."

His shoulders drop as he exhales. "I can accept that. Thank you."

"I have just one question?" I wave a finger in the air.

"What's that?"

"What on earth are we going to do about our girls?"

Chapter *seven*

Regina

"You made it." My arms go around my best friend as we sway side to side in an embrace.

After a few minutes, I pull back and take her in. Kris's braids are wound up in a bun on top of her head. Her dark brown skin looks a little dull, and the bags under her eyes tell a story I don't know the words to yet.

"How was the drive?" I ask softly.

"I don't want to see the inside of a car for a while." Her lips quirk, but the smile is lifeless.

"Seems like someone left out some pertinent details."

Kris huffs, then nods, her eyes tearing up.

"Come here, girl." I wrap her in my arms again. I don't know what's going on with her, why she felt called to move from Virginia to Holly, but I'm thankful I can be here for her.

Lord God, please bring peace to Kris's heart and comfort to her soul. Show me what she needs from me as a friend right now.

We let go, and I motion to my house. "Let me give you a quick tour." After she's seen the guest room, we make our way to the front of the house. "Kyleigh insisted we make hot cocoa for you. She's got all the potential toppings laid out and can't wait to talk your ear off."

"Good. I need to think about something other than myself."

"A road trip will mess with your thoughts when you're all alone."

"Don't I know it."

I glance at my best friend. "We'll chat later?"

She nods, and I hold back a sigh. In this type of situation, patience is the last thing I want to exercise. I want to know why the tears and find out how I can help. But Kyleigh's been looking forward to a visit from Auntie Kris since I got the phone call from her yesterday.

"Kyleigh Bear, Auntie Kris is here."

"Finally!" she shouts.

Sounds like she's in the kitchen, so I direct Kris that way. We turn the corner, and Kyleigh beams.

"Auntie Kris! You're here!" She throws her arms around Kris's waist.

She returns the hug. "I missed you, Bug."

"Me too." Kyleigh gestures to the counter. "We made you some hot cocoa. There are peppermint sticks, marshmallows, whipped cream, cinnamon, and caramel sauce. The caramel sauce and marshmallows are the best!"

Kris stares at Kyleigh in amazement. "Girlfriend, I'm impressed. Who knew a hot chocolate bar could be this fancy."

I laugh. "We're missing some other stuff, but this will have to do."

We load up our drinks and make our way to the eat-in

kitchen. Kris is awfully quiet, but Kyleigh fills the space with her chatter. When her cell rings with a call from Malea, she's off in a flash.

"She has a cell phone now?" Kris asks.

"Mother got it." I shrug a shoulder. "I didn't object. But I am enforcing time limits and making sure what she's watching is age appropriate."

"And who was the person calling her?"

"Malea." I pause. "Theo's daughter."

"What?" Kris's eyes bug out.

I have to suppress laughter because I totally get the response. Even I still can't believe I'm at a neutral setting with Theo and the world hasn't ended.

"Well, what had happened was . . ." I start, and Kris leans forward.

I spill the whole switcheroo with the girls, the Christmas concert, and the practices that have me in my feels. I end with our apologies before leaning back in my chair and taking a sip of my hot cocoa. *Whew*. I'm tired just recounting it all.

"Girl . . ." Kris breathes out. "I don't even know where to start."

"Life has been . . ." I search for the right word.

"Like you're Santa stuck in a chimney and his reindeer ditched him?"

I laugh. "Oddly specific, but, yeah, it feels like that." I jerk my chin toward Kris. "Your turn."

"No," she moans, flopping onto the table. Her arms splay out, and her forehead knocks softly against the top.

"Kris . . ." I warn.

"Fine," she mumbles, sitting up. "I saw Neil."

What's the big deal about seeing her ex-husband? She's

been divorced for as long as I've been a widow. "How? I thought he left Virginia years ago?"

"He moved back and . . ." Her eyes well up.

My heart turns over in my chest. If she's crying, something bad happened. Kris is as tough as nails. "And what?" I ask softly.

"He has a wife and a kid." The tears spill over.

My own eyes begin to water. "I'm so sorry." This has to be so difficult for her.

"I just couldn't stay. With his new position, we'd run into each other too much. And knowing he left me and got exactly what he wanted from someone else . . ." Her voice trails off.

"It's not your fault you can't have kids, and it's not your fault he's a . . ." I pause, trying to come up with a more appropriate word than the one blazing in my mind. The Lord knows I don't want to say something I'll regret, and thinking it is just as bad, but I really, *really* don't like her ex.

Kris nods anyway like she can read my mind. "He really is. You see why I needed a change of pace?"

"Definitely. You're welcome to stay here as long as you like." I hold up my hands like I'm offering my house up as a gift.

A soft smile drifts over my friend's face. "Thanks, G. I won't be a bother."

"You could never." Kris will always be the sister of my heart. The outpouring of love she showed me when Max died will forever cement her into my heart. She's family even if we don't share an ounce of blood between us.

"I think I'm going to take a nap." She hooks a finger over her shoulder. "Driving wiped me out."

"Of course. I'll wake you when dinner's ready."

"Mm." She stifles a yawn. "Thanks."

I watch as she walks down the hall, then turn my attention to my drink. Kris was meant to be a wife and mom. It's awful that her ex chose to let her go, but I can only pray a better man is still out there somewhere. I'm not sure if such a guy exists in Holly, but one can only hope.

My mind drifts to Theo and our conversation. What would've happened if I'd been more mature and told him I wanted to stay together? That trying to achieve my dream didn't mean he wasn't important?

I let out a sigh. That's foolish thinking. I can't change the past, but I can learn from it. The only question is, What lesson did God want me to learn, and how do I proceed from here?

Theo

"Dinner!" I yell through the house.

"I don't think she heard you," RJ deadpans.

I roll my eyes. "Funny. Malea's probably on the phone with Kyleigh, which means I have to compete with the noise they make while talking."

"What are you talking about?" RJ's brow furrows.

"They squeal, giggle, and ooh a lot."

RJ stares at me as if I'm the unlit bulb on a string of lights. I strain my ears to hear if she's moved, then shake my head. Malea probably hasn't budged. Cupping my mouth, I yell her name.

RJ's mouth drops. "Bro."

A thud of footsteps reaches our ears, and I give a smug smile before sitting down at the dining table.

"Sorry, Dad. I was on the phone with Kyleigh. I didn't hear you."

I give a pointed stare toward RJ.

I get it, I get it, he mouths.

"No worries, squirt. How about you say grace for us?"

"Okay." She grins, then bows her head. "Dear Lord, thank You for this food. Thank You for Uncle RJ and Dad. Thank You for Kyleigh and her mom. Thank You that we're going to do the Christmas scavenger hunt tomorrow. Amen."

"What?" I stare at my daughter, trying to make sense of her words.

"The Christmas scavenger hunt is tomorrow, Dad. How could you forget?" She shakes her head as if I'm senile and too feebleminded to keep up.

Malea grabs a roll from the bowl in the center of the table, then places it on her empty plate.

I hold up a hand. "Hold on a minute. Aren't you referring to the snow-family competition? Which isn't until Saturday, I might add."

"Nope." She stuffs her mouth full of the roll.

"Malea, I didn't sign us up for the scavenger hunt. In fact, I haven't signed us up for *any* activity." I rub the center of my forehead. "Didn't we talk about not signing me or Mrs. Parker up for any more events? You and Kyleigh can't just hijack our calendars without our permission."

"If I asked for permission, you'd say no," she pouts.

"She's got you there." RJ chews on the roast I made.

"Don't you have somewhere to be?" I say out the side of my mouth.

"Hey, you invited me." RJ turns to Malea. "Sign him up for everything. Don't forget the Christmas cookie bake-off."

"No," I moan. "I haven't done so much since . . . since . . ."

My voice trails off as I try to remember the last Christmas I was this busy with non–tree farm stuff.

"Since Mom left," Malea says quietly.

My stomach drops to my toes as I realize she's right. Have I become Jack Frost since Jianna left for Nashville?

"Yep." RJ's agreement breaks through my thoughts. "It's about time you learn the meaning of fun."

"I'm fun." My friend snorts, so I look to my daughter for help. "Malea, back me up."

"Um, you taught me not to lie."

My eyes widen. "Since when am I not fun? Didn't you try to convince Kyleigh that you have the best dad ever?"

"You are. I remember how silly you used to be, and since we've done the gingerbread competition and Christmas rehearsals, I've seen the old dad again. You even told us ridiculous Christmas jokes."

"I joke all the time."

RJ gives me a look that says *Bro, you wish.*

Wow. If Fun Dad is of the past, what kind of dad am I now?

"Please do the scavenger hunt?" Malea gives me praying hands and puppy eyes.

I'm not sure how little girls are born with the instinct to get their dads wrapped around their fingers, but I've spent the past ten years trying to build a stronger will. That look makes me want to cave, but I'm not sure I can handle being around Regina more. Yes, we apologized like grown-ups, but I *still* don't want my heart hurt. How do I know Regina will stick around Holly?

Every time we do rehearsals, I can see the love of singing still burning bright in her heart. Some parent is going to hear her practicing, videotape it on their phone, upload it to social media, then it'll go viral, and some music exec will hear how talented she is and offer her a music contract. Boom, no more Regina Parker in Holly, California.

"I'm not sure Mrs. Parker will want to." Pushing the no onto G feels a lot better than telling my kid I think I might have unresolved feelings for my ex-girlfriend.

"Kyleigh will take care of her."

A burst of laughter falls from RJ as he throws his head back. Though I'm at the butt end of the joke, I can't help but feel a twinge of humor as well. If Kyleigh is anything like Malea, G will be caving just as quickly as I'm about to.

Thinking of her as G again, huh? Sure that's smart?

"Have fun at the scavenger hunt." RJ smirks.

I ignore him and give Malea my best stern-dad face. "Make this the last activity," I warn.

"But, Dad . . ." she whines.

"I mean it. No more. We still have two more rehearsals before the concert and the snow-family competition this Saturday. Once winter break starts, you know all my time needs to go to the tree farm." As it is, I already feel stretched thin. I've had to rely on my employees to pick up my slack.

Malea's bottom lip pokes out, but she nods in agreement. "Fine."

RJ chuckles softly, and I roll my eyes before finally taking a bite of the meal *I* cooked. I'm not sure why the girls are so bent on getting me and G back together, but I hate to admit it's got me looking at Regina in a new light.

You'd be safer securing your heart tighter than gold at Fort Knox.

Because if I follow the trail my unresolved feelings are trying to lead me on, my heart might shatter like a glass ornament being batted by a cat.

Dinner goes by without any more hiccups, and soon I'm washing the dishes while RJ talks my ear off.

"You going to try and give it another go with G?" he asks.

"No," I reply quickly. "Besides, I'm pretty sure there's a rule about not dating your ex again."

"Well, it's not like you broke up with her because she was a bad person. Your dreams just took you to different places in the world. But now you guys are both in Holly. Can't be coincidence, my man."

Is he right?

"I don't know."

"Have you talked to God about it?"

I try not to fidget. I haven't really sat down and had a meaningful *be still and listen* type of moment with God. Even though I promised Malea, I've been avoiding that little bit of soul searching and made the choice to talk about things I'm ready to talk about. That's okay, right?

"Give it some thought. You can't run from your feelings forever, Theo."

"Why not?"

RJ scoffs. "Because what's in the dark will always come to light, my guy."

Shouldn't your best friend let you maintain some level of delusion? I let out the dishwater. Avoidance tactic 101.

"I mean, you don't even talk about your feelings for Jianna."

I throw a sharp look at RJ. "We're divorced. There are no more feelings."

"Sure . . ." he draws out. "You know they don't just go off like a switch, right?"

I wish they would. "At least I'm not angry anymore."

"Good, good. What else?"

I stare at him, my irritated facial expression asking if we really have to talk about our feelings.

"Yes." RJ's brows near his hairline. "Let it out."

"Fine." I huff. "I hate that Jianna barely calls Malea. She left to chase her dreams and forgot we have a child." I run a hand over my head. "Not to mention she's the second woman to leave because of some fantasy she created. Now Malea believes Regina would make a great stepmom? I don't want to burst her bubble, but G's the first woman to toss me aside for greater things. How am I supposed to let her just waltz back into my life?"

RJ folds his arms across his chest and leans against the cabinets. "Been storing that up a good while, huh?"

"Oh, I'm not done." I begin ticking the items off on my fingers. "I want a partner. Someone who will be my peace, point me to God when I need a whack upside the head, and love me like I've never been loved before. Excuse me if my heart would like to pass on attempting round two with Regina when my heart barely healed from the first go. And if I'm honest, Jianna was probably a rebound, which is *not* good, and that means I need to keep my distance from G so I don't repeat the same mistake."

I blow out a breath and run a hand down my face. My body feels like I literally just fought a battle. I'm weary, but honestly a little lighter at the same time.

"Feel better?" RJ asks after a moment or two.

"Actually?" I crack my neck left, then right. "A little bit."

"Good. Now, I guarantee God has a solution in the works. He's just waiting for you to talk to Him."

"I know you're right." I stare at my boots.

"But?"

I shrug a shoulder. "Maybe I'm afraid of His answer. I've

been guarding my heart since Jianna left. What if He tells me it's time to stop and open myself up to more hurt?"

"And what if He wants you to open up to love?" RJ claps me on the shoulder. "Go chop some more wood until you find your courage to talk to God." He pauses. "See you tomorrow?"

I nod. My words are trapped in my throat as I think about the potential responses God could have. Am I ready to lay my heart bare? But more importantly, can I handle what the Lord has to say?

Chapter *eight*

Theo

Whose bright idea was it to create a scavenger hunt that has us traipsing all over the town? There's a light dusting of snow covering the ground courtesy of last night's surprise precipitation. Which also means the air is crisp, and I want to be anywhere but at Time of Knead trying to find a gingerbread cookie.

"They have to have one," Malea says.

She looks up at me, eyes shining bright. Sometimes I see my younger face in her features, and other times I'm struck by how much Jianna is missing as our daughter continues to grow.

"You okay, Dad?"

I nod. "Yeah. Let's find that cookie."

She grins and walks inside. Regina is pretty quiet. She looks on as the girls go up to Lillian to ask about the scavenger hunt. She hands over a cookie in a plastic bag, and the girls cheer. If they're this excited over the first item on the list, I wonder how they'll feel when we get to the end of the list.

"There's no way that enthusiasm carries throughout the contest," Regina mutters.

I let out a laugh. "My thoughts exactly. Kids, they're overly eager the first ten minutes, then get bored and whine the rest of the time."

"Real." She sighs. "Sometimes I wish I could dab that energy on like perfume and let it infuse my body."

"Wow, going all Sanderson sisters on the little children?"

A genuine smile appears on G's face, and my heart flops in my chest. It's almost like that little jolt your car gets when you jump a dead battery for the first time. Not to say I'm dead inside, but . . . you get the picture.

Malea directs us to the coffee shop for the next clue. I naturally fall behind the girls, and Regina soon matches my steps.

"I'm not trying to suck out their souls. Just borrow some energy so I don't fall into my bed exhausted at nine p.m. like a little ol' lady."

"I get that. Who knew being a single parent would have you itching for a nap or some time alone?"

"Yes!" G's eyes get wide. "I love Kyleigh, but what I wouldn't give for five minutes of silence. When she gets started on a subject she loves . . ." Regina shakes her head. "I need favor from the Lord because I want to cut her off so badly."

"But you don't want to stifle her spirit, so you listen as she goes on ad nauseum."

"Oh, Malea is the same way?"

I nod. "She's always had a lot to say. It was cute when she was two and it all sounded like gibberish, but at five I was playing the silent game to get a reprieve."

"Smart."

The girls get a stirrer, then they're off racing to the next business. I'm not sure when Regina and I silently agreed to trail behind them, but we do. The glowing lights, the crisp air, the low tone of our voices, all makes for an intimate atmosphere. Holly's Main Street is showing off in all its festive glory. All we're missing is music to up the atmosphere off the charts.

We watch as the girls find another item, and Regina and I keep following behind them. I'm not sure if I should switch the subject to something depressing to make sure I don't turn into a sappy fool or let the conversation naturally evolve like it's been.

"What do you do on the days when it feels too hard to be a single parent?" Regina bites her lip and studies me.

I face forward, thinking of her question. "Honestly, those are the days I ask the Lord for a double portion to get through the day. I figure on a good day, I just need a regular portion, but on those kind of days . . ." I exhale. "Yeah, a double portion and a whole heaping of grace is needed."

"Glad to hear you still talk about God and prayer so casually. It was always the thing that made you different from the rest of the guys," Regina says softly.

Wow. She was attracted to my faith? It's not something she ever complimented me on in the past, but the warm feeling spreading in my chest tells me it's something I needed to hear.

"I'm far from perfect," I warn, thinking of how I've been avoiding the deep stuff with the Lord.

She snorts. "You being perfect never entered my mind."

"Ouch, G. Give a guy a little warning before you stab him in the back." The nickname slips out before I can correct, but her laughter fills the air. Despite being at the opposite end of her joke, I'm grinning right along with her.

"You know what I mean. No one is perfect, and I'm not trying to put you on a pedestal or anything. Just saying thank you for living out your faith genuinely."

"Appreciate that." Good thing guys don't blush. That heat rising up the back of my neck is all from the exertion of scavenger hunting and nothing more.

Our conversation continues as the kids go from business to business, finding each item on the list.

"We're done!" Malea shouts after the last item is crossed off. She runs toward me.

"Don't run," I caution. Who knows where black ice is hiding?

She slows, then shakes the scavenger hunt paper at me. "We found everything. We gotta beat everyone back and win the prize."

Kyleigh bobs her head in agreement. I direct the girls back to the chamber of commerce, who hosts the yearly game. But when we get there, we're not the first in line. We're the second.

"Aw, man," Kyleigh whispers.

I squeeze her shoulder. "Doesn't mean you guys didn't do well."

Kyleigh looks up at me for a second, then glances away. "Yeah, means someone did better," she grumbles.

Regina's shoulder shakes as if she's stifling a laugh.

The family in front of us leaves, and we turn in our paper and all the items we found.

"Congratulations!" the woman behind the desk says. "You're the second group to finish up."

"We wanted to be first," Malea states.

"Well, you didn't win the grand prize, but I do have a second-place prize for you."

Both of the girls perk up and lean forward. She hands over a gift card to one of the local restaurants. "Enjoy a meal on us."

"Thanks!" Malea smiles.

We exit the building, and I look at my ex. "Guess I'll see you at rehearsal tomorrow?"

"Guess so."

I wave awkwardly, then do an about-face. Malea walks in step with me.

"You need to learn how to flirt," she says after a moment.

"You're killing me, squirt."

"Someone has to teach you the ways."

I let out a chuckle, then tug her to my side. "Let's get you home and in bed before you can stir up more trouble."

"There's always tomorrow."

Man, I love this cheeky kid.

Regina

"Hey, Mom, can I talk to you?"

I pause my movie as my daughter walks toward my bed. "Of course you can, Kyleigh Bear." I pat the empty spot next to me in my bed.

If my daughter wants to chat, I'll make time for her. Every. Single. Time.

She curls up next to me, and I wrap an arm around her shoulder. "What's up?"

"I was just thinking about Dad. Tell me how you met again?"

I rest my chin against the top of her head. "We bumped into each other outside of the humanities building on campus. I was leaving, and he was coming in." I smile, remembering how much Max mumbled while trying to pick up my notebook and textbook that scattered to the ground. "It was like most of the Hallmark meet-cutes. We just bumped into each other, and the rest is history."

"Do you miss him a whole lot? Did you love him so much you'll never marry again?" she asks quietly.

My heart twists at the sadness in her voice. "We were married for a couple of years before he died. I will always miss him and hate that he doesn't get to see you grow up." My throat aches at the thought. Max would've loved every single thing about Kyleigh. How intelligent she is, how kind she is. Everything that makes her *her* would've had him brimming with pride.

"Will you ever date again?"

I squeeze my eyes shut. Part of me wants her to forget the question, especially knowing how she's trying to maneuver Theo Evers back into my world.

"I don't know, sweetie. I imagine that when I meet the right man, God will let me know it's safe to try again." Safe. Funny how that's the word that left my mouth.

"What about Mr. Evers? How did you two meet? Did you have a meet-cute with him too?"

I snort. "No. I've known him since kindergarten. Holly is small and not a lot of people move here. All the adults who live here now, well, most of them I grew up with."

"Then what made you want to date him?"

Probably the fact I had a crush on him even in my earliest memories. Theo was my childhood, but I can't explain all those intricacies to Kyleigh. Besides, she just wants to know what changed. "In our junior year of high school, a couple of weeks before the homecoming game and dance, Theo invited me to his house to hang out. When I showed up he had a piece of wood, just a little circle, but it had our initials carved into a heart. He looked me in the eyes and asked me to Homecoming."

Chills go up my arms, and I'm thankful my robe covers the telltale signs. The memory sparks a flush in my cheeks that I don't want to analyze. Don't want to admit just how much my heart palpitates at the memory.

"Did you say yes?"

"Mm-hmm." I need to get my emotions under control before I can speak again.

"Was Homecoming your first date?"

I nod, flushing at the memories.

"What *is* Homecoming?" Kyleigh asks.

A soft chuckle escapes me, then I explain what it is.

"Wow, so I have to wait until high school to go to a dance?"

"Nah, I believe dances start in middle school. But most middle schoolers are too afraid to go to them." I hug her tightly. Hopefully she's a long way away from dating. *She's ten. You started dating at sixteen. That's in six years.* The thought has me holding her even tighter.

"Most people or you?"

I laugh outright. "Good question. Not sure."

"What song did you dance to?"

My face burns. If I tell her, will it give her more ideas? But if I don't, will she just imagine the most romantic song anyway?

"Why does it matter?" I ask instead.

"Just curious. I like learning stuff about you."

Oof. This girl knows how to hit me right in the heart. "It was 'Love Story.'"

"Taylor Swift?" she squeals.

My girl is a self-proclaimed Swiftie, so her excitement doesn't surprise me.

"That's a great song."

"Mm." But she's not wrong. For a while that song was *our* song. It became our makeup song for when we got in an argument (there were many—remember, maturity of a mosquito). But when we had our big argument, I stopped listening to "Love Story" *and* Taylor Swift. No offense to her, but just hearing her voice made me tear up for the longest time.

Does that mean I have unresolved issues with Theo? Because seeing him again, remembering the words we exchanged, getting a sincere apology from him, all of it seems to be crumbling my walls and breaking me down bit by bit. I'm not sure what to do with the emotions rising in me.

"'Night, Mom." Kyleigh shifts away and kisses me on my cheek before she hops out of the bed.

"'Night, Kyleigh Bear."

I stare at the rom-com frozen on my TV. Over the years, I've watched romance after romance, oohing and aahing over the couple and their journey to happily ever after. But when did I stop believing I could have a similar journey? A breakup with my high school sweetheart. The death of my husband. That equals tragedy for all relationships, doesn't it?

Lord, what do I do? I don't know how to feel about Theo. Correction, I know how I feel, but I don't want to feel this way. I want you to just wipe my emotions, my memories with Theo Evers, clean.

Maybe if God wipes the slate, I can start at a new friendship with Theo instead of remembering all the ways my future turned out differently than I planned. Maybe that little voice inside my heart will stop suggesting that we still have time to change our future.

Chapter *nine*

Regina

How did I find myself outside the Holly Christmas tree farm? I glance at the person sitting in the back seat, bouncing with glee. Oh yeah, my child, that's right. However, picking out a Christmas tree has always been part of our holiday tradition, so I couldn't say no. Fortunately, Kris is with me. I'm hoping she'll act as some kind of buffer if—*Lord, please let it be an* if—I run into Theo.

"Let's go find our tree," I say.

"Yes!" Kyleigh exits the back seat.

Kris and I follow, exchanging amused glances as I lock the car.

The air is a little nippy, but nothing terrible. My peacoat is the perfect buffer against the cold and stylish enough that *if* I run into Theo, I won't feel like the Stay Puft Marshmallow Man like I would've if I wore my puffer jacket.

When will you stop thinking about Theo and what he thinks about you? Surely, he doesn't care what kind of jacket you wear.

Still, I can't stop myself from overanalyzing the clothes in my closet whenever the possibility of a Theo sighting comes into the forecast. My lilac slouch beanie is giving me an extra-cute vibe, so I can scope out our tree and not fear I look like a troll.

"Mom, can we have some cider?" Kyleigh points to the stand that sells hot drinks.

"Sure. Do you want a snack too?"

Her head bobs up and down vigorously. She gets her sweet tooth from me.

"Kris?" I ask.

"Definitely." She smiles.

I'm relieved the bags under her eyes aren't as prominent as when she arrived. Hopefully a few more restful nights will have them gone completely. Not sure what the remedy for a broken heart is though.

Keep praying for her.

"I want the Christmas pinwheel sugar cookie." Kyleigh looks up at me with a puppy dog stare.

"I already agreed to get you a snack. Lay off the cutie eyes."

She grins, and I hold back a sigh. This age has me in the feels more often than not. Kyleigh still has the chubby cheeks of youth and doesn't have all her permanent teeth in yet. But I can see her slimming down here and there, and that early tween look is coming out. I'm not ready for the teenage years, but time is going by way too fast. If I were to wrap her in a hug, she might accuse me of smothering her.

Who cares?

I grab Kyleigh and squeeze her close, peppering her face with kisses.

"Mom . . ." Somehow she turns the word into three syllables.

"I love you, Kyleigh Bear."

She stops squirming, and her arms go around my waist. "I love you too," she whispers.

The person in front of us leaves, and I let go of my daughter and place our order. I end up paying for three apple ciders, two Christmas pinwheels, and a chocolate-covered pretzel stick (that one is all mine). We'll all be on a sugar high, but my justification is the calories we're about to burn looking for a tree. Does traipsing through the woods mean I should have *two* pretzel sticks?

Nah, one is enough.

We meander away from the stand, food and drink in hand. "Want to pick out a tree now?" I ask.

"No." Kyleigh shakes her head. "Let's go make a wreath. Remember the old one broke?"

"Wait, y'all can make wreaths here?" Kris asks.

I nod. Kyleigh's right. We pulled out decorations last night to see what we're working with, and my wreath snapped in half when I dropped it on accident. Who knew it would be so flimsy?

We head to the red barn on Theo's property. I look around with new—a.k.a. non-bitter—eyes to take in all he's done. There's a tractor pulling kids in a trailer that's been converted to a winter wonderland. Families sit on snow mounds as miniature snowmen and reindeer decorate the other spaces. There are also various food stands, picnic tables, and activities around the barn to create homemade décor. Not to mention a lighted path of white lights leading toward the trees for sale.

It's kind of magical, and I can't help feeling a twinge of pride for Theo. He did what he always wanted to do. If I had supported his dream, would I have been able to attain mine as well? Working with the kids for the Christmas concert has me slowly singing again at home. Every time Kyleigh catches me, her grin is so big I'm beginning to realize how important it is for her to hear me sing.

When Max died, part of me stopped believing in happy endings. Which begs the question, If I'm singing a little here and there, does that mean my subconscious is starting to believe, even if I can't consciously fathom it?

When we step inside the barn, there are a bunch of tables covered with materials to make various crafts. We find an empty one and grab the supplies to construct a wreath. We're so preoccupied with the activity that I jump when a deep voice interrupts us.

"Well, if it isn't little Regina Childs."

Hand over my heart, I whirl around to take in the six-feet-two-inch man in front of me. "RJ Griggs. Look who turned into a mountain man."

He grins, his brown lips framed by an impressive beard. RJ used to be the runt in our friend group, but it looks like hanging out on the tree farm has benefited him.

"How've you been?" I ask, now that my pulse is steady.

"Good. My parents moved to Phoenix for the year-round warm weather, and I took over their place."

"Their house or their business?" The Griggs have run the coffee shop on Main since as long as I can remember.

"The Daily Grind too. I have a good manager who runs the place when Theo needs help chopping trees and whatnot. What about you? I thought I saw you opened something up on Main too."

I nod. "Scents and Sensibility. It's a candle shop."

"Clever."

Kris clears her throat, and I remember my manners.

"RJ, this is my friend Kris Latimore. Kris, this is RJ. I grew up with him."

They exchange greetings, and then RJ looks at me once more. "Theo told me about the switch-up." He jerks his chin toward Kyleigh, and his lips twitch with barely suppressed mirth.

"Laugh it up, funny man. Do you have kids?"

"No." He holds up his hands in the clearest *no way* sign I've ever seen. "That's not for me."

"Scared of them?" Kris asks.

He scoffs. "More like sufficiently cautious."

"You can always babysit for me, then." Though my mother does most of the babysitting. It's not like I actually need to ask her to look after Kyleigh. My mother doesn't need any prompting to see her grandchild, and I don't date.

Wow, that's a depressing thought.

"I see you still got jokes, G."

This is what I've been missing: friendship. I don't know why I moved back home to Holly for all things familiar only to isolate myself and ignore the things that make Holly Holly, which includes the people.

"I try," I say.

"Yo, RJ."

We all turn at the sound of Theo's voice. He strides across the barn, a look of consternation on his face. My heart stutters at the cream Henley he's wearing. It hugs every muscle in his arms and torso. Seriously, it's not fair that Theo has aged so well. There's no signs of a dad bod or premature balding. It's wholly unfair, yet my eyes don't object to anything they're seeing.

My pulse gallops like I'm on a sleigh ride, and all I want to do is get closer to—Or is that farther from?—the man causing havoc with my emotions. I avert my gaze, only to catch the knowing look on Kris's face.

Theo? she mouths.

I nod.

"You're in trouble," she murmurs.

Theo

RJ has been my best friend since elementary school. He's one of the best men I know, and I'm lucky he puts up with my grumpy ways. Yet seeing Regina smiling and laughing with him and knowing she's not that way with me sends a wave of longing through me. And a little bit of jealousy. Not the kind that makes me want to bang my chest and mark my territory, but the kind that makes me think, *Please let your guard down with me too.*

"Yo, RJ." The words rip from my throat before I can stop them. I have no idea what to say. I can't even remember the reason I walked into the barn.

"Everything okay?" Regina asks. "I've never seen lines so deeply etched into a forehead." She smirks to let me know she's joking.

But it's not a laugh. Her eyes aren't smiling the way she was a second ago with my best friend.

Maybe she needs more time to believe you're sorry for your part in the breakup.

I've known G about as long as I've known RJ. I used to know every single thing about her. However, the woman before me has changed, and I'm not sure she's willing to open up and let me get to know the current version.

Do you want *to know her?* More importantly, do I want a second chance with her? If so, I have to do the work.

"Uh, I was thinking," I stammer out. *Not cool.* I'm tongue-tied and awkward. If I turn around and walk away, will that make me seem like a jerk, or will she think I'm merely moody? *But that leaves her with RJ.*

Regina nods. "Oh, this is my friend Kris. Kris, Theo." She gestures to a woman who has her hair in long braids. They're tossed behind her as she wrestles with a miniature foam tree to decorate.

"Nice to meet you."

"Likewise. I've heard a lot about you."

I'm not sure if that's a good thing, but curiosity sparks anyway. If G's talking about me, that means she's thinking about me. Again, not sure if that's a good thing, but I'll liken it to publicity—you know, no such thing as bad publicity. If she's thinking about me, I'll take it.

"Where's Malea?" Regina looks over my shoulder as if my daughter will materialize from thin air.

"Last I saw, she was on the tractor pull. Haven't seen her since."

"Boo." Kyleigh pokes her lip out.

"There she is." RJ points behind Regina, and we all swing our heads that way.

"Malea!" Kyleigh shouts, cupping her mouth.

My daughter spies her best friend, and her eyes light up. She takes in the scene, and I can see a calculating look slide into her gaze. If a game show host asks me to stare at pairs of eyes and identify my child, that calculating look will give her away each time. Thank the Lord there's not two of her.

"Hey." Malea waves at everyone, then sees the blank

wreath on the table. "Oh, cool, are you guys making a wreath?"

"Want to join us?" Regina asks. She glances at me, as if to ask if that's okay.

I give a slight nod, and she turns back to Malea, who's already cheering.

"Hey, squirt, why don't you grab another wreath so we can hang it at home when you're done?"

"Okay, Dad!" She runs to Melissa and grabs materials for another wreath.

"Do you want to join us?" Regina asks me.

I do, but *should* I is the better question.

"He does," RJ responds.

He nudges me with his sharp elbow, and I grunt. "Yeah, that'll be nice."

"Don't say yes on my account, Scrooge."

I study Regina to see if she's being playful or if there's any seriousness behind her words. Her expression gives nothing away, and I'm left to make a decision: say something snarkier or smirk. I go with option B, and I'm rewarded with a dip of her head and a whisper of a smile on her lips.

Who knew saying sorry would change the tide between us so quickly? I'm grateful God got ahold of my prideful nature and shook it loose. I don't want to be at odds with Regina, not when I can't help but think of all the good things in our past.

The girls guide us in making the wreath as we sip on drinks. At one point, Kris offers to take the girls for another snack run.

Regina gestures around the barn and looks at me in amazement. "This is fantastic, Theo. Looks like your dreams came true."

"Kind of." I cock my head to the side. "What about you? What happened to singing on Broadway?"

Judging by the way she's looking away, embarrassment is filling her up, and that's not my intent. "No judgment," I say gently. "Just want to catch up on your life."

"Okay." She lets out a breath. "I met Kyleigh's father in college. When I graduated with my degree, he was getting ready to go to law school. He proposed and I said yes. We got married, and I ended up putting my Broadway dreams on hold so we could move down to Virginia, where he'd been accepted into law school."

That must have broken her heart. She loves singing more than anything . . . or at least she used to.

"When I got pregnant with Kyleigh, Max thought it would be great if I'd stay home, so I did. I made candles and sold them online, and when Max passed away, I poured every ounce of free time into my online candle shop to support us."

"Now you own a store."

She grins. "And now I own a store. It's not singing, it's not what I imagined for my life. But it's so much better. Every time Kyleigh smiles at me, I have no regrets. I wouldn't trade her for all the Tony Awards in the world."

I have no doubt she could win one. Her voice is that amazing, and she always made me believe in her acting. Getting to hear her coach the kids during practice has been an honor. "I'm happy for you."

"What about you? This place offers so much more than Christmas trees."

Looking around the barn, I try to see it through fresh eyes. There are a lot of families at each of the tables making wreaths and other décor. Laughter rings out as the

Christmas music pipes in from the sound system I have throughout the property.

"You know, it's an idea that came to me when I was chopping wood one day."

Her mouth drops. "You really chop wood?"

"I do own a tree farm."

She chuckles and shakes her head as if saying *Of course.* "Right. That makes sense. Also explains the muscles." She grabs her cheeks à la Kevin McCallister. "Kill me now. I did *not* say that out loud."

"No, no. I'm all ears. Should I flex for you?" I make a show of doing so, and the embarrassment all over her face wars with appreciation.

She laughs, covering her mouth, and I realize I really am willing to be a fool for Regina Parker. The feeling welling inside is almost the same as when we were teens. Back then, I wanted to win every smile, every laugh. Now I'm making ridiculous body-building poses because of the sounds of joy filling the air. Looks like I'll be talking to God about my feelings after all.

By the time the ladies return, G's wiping tears away. Malea glances back and forth between us while Kyleigh beams. And Kris, well, her expression is unreadable. I don't know her well enough to guess but just seeing her assessing the situation has me straightening up and leaving my poses behind. The girls do some ridiculous handshake, and I have a feeling they may be on the right track with throwing Regina and me back together.

Chapter *ten*

Theo

Today's the snow-family competition. We're in the back lot of Outdoor Adventures, the adventure company that does hikes and all sorts of activities in Holly and around the county. They're hosting the twenty-fifth annual snow-family competition. Artificial snow has been piped in, Christmas goodies are at the snack table near the shop, and families are grouped together near mounds of snow.

Malea and Kyleigh chat animatedly while Regina stands near me, jostling left to right.

"Cold?" I ask.

"Hm?" She glances at me and freezes. With a slow blink, she shakes her head. "Uh, no. I just don't want to get cold. Once they start the competition, I'll be fine. No way I'll freeze building a snow family."

"Are we building them like us?" I motion to the four of us. "I mean, I assume so, but you know what they say about assumptions. 'Ask questions, don't make assumptions.'"

"Your grandma always said that." Regina smiles.

"Yep, like us." Malea points to Kyleigh. "We've already picked out clothes for our snowmen."

"Come again?" G asks.

"Don't worry. We got this." The girls give us thumbs-ups.

Before I can say anything further, Mal with Outdoor Adventures calls for our attention. It's funny to see him run his own business when I remember how unmotivated he was in high school. He gives us the rules, the time limit, and introduces the judges. Then a foghorn blares, and we're off gathering snow. Malea and Kyleigh inform Regina and me we're each responsible for building our own snowman.

If history has taught me anything, it's that Regina can't roll a snowball to save her life. And judging from her paltry attempts now, she hasn't improved. I say nothing and instead roll up a snowman until I have one my height.

"How do you do that?" Regina eyes me with envy.

"Ask nicely and I'll make yours."

She bites her lip, looking completely kissable. *Slow your roll, Evers. You haven't even asked her out.*

My body jolts. Is that what I want? To date Regina again? I search my thoughts and realize that's exactly what I want to do.

But what about your heart? Don't you want to keep it safe?

Maybe so, but the happiest I've ever been in life is with Regina. Yes, there have been other moments of happiness. After all, being Malea's dad has been the best thing ever. But in the romantic arena, Regina has always been my person.

"Will you please make mine?" Regina fakes fluttering her

lashes, having no clue it's making my pulse flutter right along.

I give her a slow grin in return. "Yes, I'll make yours."

Rolling the base for her snowperson, my mind moves about the same pace as I contemplate asking Regina out. *Lord, you know how I feel. You know all the emotions I've been trying to ignore as well as the pain and hurt I've been trying to prevent. But I know You ask me to trust You and seek You first. So here I am. Should I ask Regina out?*

Who knew rolling snowballs to match the height of the woman I like would be a great time for prayer? As I share all my worries with the Lord, I shift from anxious to calm.

Should I just come right out and ask her? Should I make sure the kids aren't in hearing distance? No telling how they'll react. They might think they can orchestrate chaos all the time and it will turn out just as they imagine.

Adding the last ball, I stand back to examine Regina's snowperson. It's right next to mine—placed there at the girls' bidding—and behind Kyleigh's, which is next to Malea's, who made her snowman in front of mine.

"Now what?" I ask.

"Now we dress them." Malea looks at me as if to say, *You know nothing.*

It's the same expression she's been giving me since she could talk. Somehow, someway, my child has been here before. She's got this sense and wisdom that belongs to someone much older, yet it's trapped in a ten-year-old body. However, just when I'm convinced she's older than her biological age, she starts talking about brain rot, and I'm wholly aware she's a Gen Alpha kid and I'm not as young as I used to be.

The girls grab the duffel bag and unzip it, pulling out

clothes that suspiciously resemble something from my closet. I thought the girls brought a scarf or two. Nope. Malea drapes my snowman with *my* suit jacket. Then they drape a prom dress on the front of Regina's snowwoman, looping a satin sash around the waist to hold it up. My brow furrows in confusion as they pin a corsage to the snowwoman. Next the snowgirls are outfitted with frilly dresses as well.

What happened to winter clothing? At least everyone gets a carrot nose and some black buttons for eyes.

Regina walks toward me and folds her arms. "You know what this is, right?"

"No, why? Do you understand the look they're going for?"

"Mm-hmm. You don't see it?"

I study the snow family, trying to get the picture. Before I can admit ignorance, Malea takes out her cell phone and plays a song. I freeze as strands of "Love Story" greet my ear.

"Ah, you finally figured it out," Regina says softly.

I nod wordlessly. The girls have recreated the year that changed everything for me. Homecoming with the one girl I always wanted in my life. How did they know? Did Regina tell them?

Our kids are wearing twin hopeful expressions, and having G stand so near makes me want to drop my armor and be completely transparent. Guarding my heart against the one woman who's always made my heart come alive seems ridiculous, especially now that apologies have been given. Because now I know I'd give anything for another chance with Regina Parker.

Turning, I face the woman who held my heart in her hands when I was a teen and stare into her beautiful eyes. "G," I say quietly. "Will you go out with me?"

Her eyes widen as she takes in the seriousness of my expression. She opens her mouth and—

The foghorn rends the air, and we all jump at the sound. My heart pounds in my ears as I turn toward Mal, who looks at all the contestants with a sheepish grin.

"Sorry about that. Probably should've given you a vocal warning before giving y'all heart attacks."

"Guess that's why I have a pacemaker," Sam, one of the Holly residents, yells out.

I chuckle, but my palms are sweaty. Regina didn't answer me, and now I'm too afraid to look at her. Will I get rejected once more? Will she deem me unworthy again?

Don't. Don't base your worth on the women who leave. Because I *know* my worth is based on God's love. It's just so hard to hold on to that when people you love keep leaving. I want to believe that Regina won't leave again, but the way my brain is yelling, *Retreat, retreat!*, means I don't quite believe it. Still, I don't want to take back my question because I'm dying on the inside waiting for her answer.

Mal walks around and judges the snow families. We don't win, but we're awarded a ribbon for Best Dressed, which has the girls squealing in delight.

Mal stops in front of Regina and me. "Never thought I'd see the two of you back together again."

"Oh, we're not . . ." Regina's voice trails off.

My face heats, and I speak to get us out of the awkward situation. "Our daughters are best friends. We're merely enjoying the festivities."

Mal's eyes squint. "Yeah. Sure."

Then he continues walking as if he didn't nail awkwardness to the wall. Instead of turning to face G—who I *know* is staring because she's burning a hole in my cheek—I clap my hands and call for my daughter.

"Time to go. The tree farm waits for no man or girl."

"Ah, Dad. Can't I hang out with Kyleigh for just a little bit longer?"

I rub a hand across my chin, mentally thinking of the drive back and forth from the town proper and our property. "I'm not sure I have the time."

"I do," Regina offers. "I can bring her home after dinner, if that's okay with you."

Malea clasps her hands and gives me a pleading look. I'm caving before I even swing my gaze back to G. "Thanks. I appreciate that."

She nods. "And maybe we can finish our conversation then?"

My breath hitches. She's not shooting me down?

I stare deep into her eyes. "I'd like that."

Regina

The girls chatter all the way back to my house, but I don't hear a single word they say. Instead, my mind is full of Theo, the snowmen setup that reminded me of our first date, and the question that followed.

"G, will you go out with me?"

Even now, the memory sends a flurry of awareness through me. Maybe I'm not actually a stranger to romance. Although it *has* been a while since I've entertained the idea of dating or being in a relationship. With Theo, it's not just what could be but also the reminder of what was.

When we were together in high school, life was good.

Theo was attentive. Made me feel cared for and safe. Not to mention the feelings between us made me think fireworks.

I'm just not sure how that looks in my mid-thirties. Marrying Max brought me a cozy life. And once I found my footing after his passing, life became stable once more. Am I willing to risk that stability for something with the man who never gave me steady? The only thing dependable about Theo when we dated was knowing he loved me and would show up. Everything else felt electric. Then again, he has matured. What's more stable than running a tree farm and raising a child? And new Theo doesn't provoke me just for laughs. But the real question is, Can I risk more potential loss?

"Mom, did you hear me?"

I shake my head and stare at my daughter. "Sorry. I was in my own world. What did you say?"

"Can we watch *Frozen* one and two and have cookies?"

"Sure. You want me to join you guys?" I'm never sure if Kyleigh wants me around or wants the space to just be with her friends.

"Yes, please," Malea says with a quick grin.

"All right. Ready the room and I'll get cookies and drinks."

"Ready the room?" Malea questions.

"I'll show you." Kyleigh takes Malea over to the ottoman that holds our blankets for movie time.

Knowing she's got that covered, I open the cookie tin that has the sugar cookies we made last night. Kris helped, and she actually laughed for the first time since she arrived. Which reminds me . . .

I pull out my cell and text her. I'm not sure if she's napping or wants to be alone, but maybe she wants to join in for movie night.

Regina
Want to watch Frozen? It's a girls' night with Kyleigh and Malea.

Kris
Is Theo here too?

My cheeks heat at the question.

Regina
No, just his daughter.

Kris
There's a story here. I'll be out in a sec. Are pajamas permitted?

Regina
Pajamas are standard.

I call out to Kyleigh and make sure she knows to change into some pjs and offer a set to Malea. Soon we're all gathered in the living room with piles of blankets covering our legs, and *Frozen* playing on the screen. The platter of cookies lies next to the platter of Christmas-flavored popcorn (red-and-green sprinkles on kettle corn). Cider was faster to make than cocoa, so I served everyone a mug of the spiced liquid.

"How did this become a Christmas movie?" Kris whispers.

I shrug. "Because it's cold?"

She snickers.

The girls break out singing, and I hum along. The Christmas concert is in a few days, and the students have done a wonderful job. It's also made me realize just how much I miss singing, which means I've started singing and humming to myself more.

That's also probably why Kris is nudging me with her elbow, trying to get me to lean over so she can find out about the sudden change.

"Don't ignore me, G," she warns mockingly.

I sigh. "I miss singing."

"Good. It's a shame not to use the talent God gave you."

My face burns. Did I turn into the "wicked, lazy servant" from the parable? The thought sends trembles of fear to my core. "Have I squandered my talent?"

"Oh, honey." Kris's gaze softens, and she squeezes my hand. "Your heart's been wounded for a really long time. Sometimes we're in a dormant season and not a season of purposely being disobedient. You've been healing as God pruned the dead things in order for the living fruit to multiply. I think your singing is finally entering its blooming season."

Tears appear. Before I can blink them back, they spill over. Kris passes a napkin to me and faces forward, giving me time to compose myself. She's right. I *have* been wounded. I'm not sure why I ignored the fact I'm still hurting, but I don't want to anymore. I want to enter the land of the living again instead of just going through the motions. I want to enjoy my time with Kyleigh, Kris, and anyone else that God brings into my life.

Like Theo?

My heart quickens, and before I can change my mind, I open my text messages and find his number.

Regina

Yes

Theo

I don't want to jump to conclusions but . . .

My lips curve into a smile. I type up a longer reply.

Regina
Yes, I would like to go on a date with you, Theo Evers.

Theo
You just made my night.

Chapter *eleven*

Regina

Since the girls switched places, I've spent too much time in front of my closet trying to figure out what to wear. What used to be acceptable attire now seems drab and lifeless. My wardrobe looks like it belongs to a woman who has no clue how to wear clothes but knows she needs them and grabs the first thing she sees.

A soft chuckle sounds behind me, and I turn to see Kris walk into the room.

"What?"

"Can't figure out what to wear on your date?" she sing-songs the last word.

My hands immediately touch my hot face. "Girl, I'm in over my head," I mutter through my squished cheeks.

"No, you're not. You're too in your head. Just stop thinking so much."

"How do I do that?"

Kris shrugs a shoulder. "When I figure that out, I'll let you know."

We've spent plenty of nights together overthinking and spiraling before we snapped each other out of our doomsday thoughts.

"Still"—I gesture to my clothes—"what do I wear?"

"Where is he taking you?"

"He wants it to be a surprise. Just told me to dress warmly."

"Sounds like an outdoor date, then." Kris taps her chin. "Hmm. What is there to do in Holly outdoors?"

I shrug, but then I sink onto my bed to think. What *is* there to do? "Drive around and look at the lights?"

"For a date?"

"That's something we would've done in high school."

"Yeah, because you probably didn't have a lot of money." Kris snorts and sits in the chair across from my bed.

"Ice skating?" I say hesitantly.

"Ooh, that's romantic. At least it looks that way in the movies. I'm not sure the idea of falling on my butt and freezing outside makes my heart pitter patter."

I chuckle. "Yeah, you're definitely the dinner-and-a-movie type."

"So are you." Kris laughs.

"Maybe, but I wouldn't be horrified if a guy tried to take me hiking or—" I break off because she's shuddering, and it's the funniest thing ever. That or I'm tired from the long workday and slightly loopy.

When we both stop laughing, Kris stares deeply into my eyes. "G, it's okay to date again. It's okay to have fun. It's okay to dress girly or comfortable or however you like. It's okay to be you and let Theo get to know the new you."

My throat thickens with unshed tears. How did she address all of my worries? "Thanks." I dab at the corner of my eye.

"God's got you."

"I know He does. He's been with me every step of the way, especially these past ten years." I pause to gather the courage to say what I'm really afraid of. "But what if God believes that Theo isn't for me? That this ship has sailed, and, instead of something fun, this becomes one more tragedy in my story?"

"Then you trust that He *still* has great plans for you." Kris leans forward. "I hate that I'm divorced and how Neil treated me like I'm broken. The only thing getting me up every morning is knowing God has something better. I don't know when that time is and I certainly don't know what those great plans entail, but I believe. And on the days when my faith seems to waver, God reminds me of why I should keep believing."

The words are convicting, but they're also so very encouraging. Who knew I needed a reason to believe again this Christmas season? It seems poignant that in the time Christians around the world are celebrating the birth of Jesus—even if He probably was born in the summer—that God is giving me a reminder that I need to believe goodness can wait for me in my future.

I get up and open my arms for a much-needed hug. Kris feels tiny in my arms, and I'm aware of how much weight she's lost. I pull back and look in her eyes. "Have you had lunch?"

"Okay, Mom. But, yes, I had some leftover loaded baked potato soup."

Relief fills me. "Good."

She pats me on the back. "I'm better now. Promise." She points to the closet. "Now pick something out and get dressed. What time will he be here?"

I glance at my watch. "Thirty minutes."

"Then you better hurry."

I'm kind of low maintenance, so I don't need a huge amount of time to get ready, but I also don't want to feel like I'm rushing. Moving back to my closet, I reach for some black jeggings—because comfort masquerading as cute—and then I pick out a red cable-knit sweater. I spin my rotating jewelry holder—okay, so I like earrings, sue me—and find the red mitten pair with snowflakes on them. After adding some blush, lipstick, and mascara I'm all set. My hair still has leftover curls from yesterday. The only thing I can't decide is which jacket to wear. If we're outside for the entire evening, should I wear my parka?

We've been inundated with gusts of wind the last two days that make it feel purely arctic in my opinion. Still, we warmed back up to fifty this afternoon. Perhaps the parka is unnecessary. *You know you want to wear the peacoat for the cuteness factor.* Right, I'm wearing what I want, so peacoat it is. By the time I make it to the front of the house, the doorbell rings.

Immediately, my cheeks heat. Instead of pretending I'm not blushing, I give in to it. I like Theo. Liking him has never been a problem. Now I have a second chance to see if there can be anything lasting between us. I'm going to trust God like Kris advised and pray this is a perfect date. I open the door, and the sight of Theo holding a stuffed snowman and wearing a nervous expression melts me right away. Tonight's going to be a good night.

Theo

I stare into Regina's beautiful face, and my throat instantly clogs with emotion. *Lord God, please don't let me mess up this second chance.* I really believe that G and I can go the distance if that spark is still there. Seems like the only thing standing in our way is ourselves, and I don't want to be the foolish man I was in the past.

Taking a deep breath, I speak. "You look beautiful."

She grins, and I offer the stuffed snowman I found in one of the shops on Main. Regina used to collect them, not sure if she still does, but it made me think of her.

"You remembered," she says softly.

"Of course I did."

"I know just where to put him. One sec." She rushes to an armchair that has a pillow shaped like a snowflake. She places the snowman in front of the pillow, then comes back to the door, stepping outside.

"He's perfect. Thanks, Theo." Regina looks up at me. "Where are we going?"

"Food first, then fun."

"Sounds like a plan."

I offer my elbow. What I really want to do is hold her hand, but we both have on gloves, so that'll have to wait. After I shut the car door, my mind begins to race. What do I say to her? Will talking to her be as easy as it was in high school or more difficult now that we're adults? I hate that I don't know, but I've spent too much time praying to worry now. God's got this, even if I somehow manage to make us crash and burn once more.

The heat greets me as I climb into the driver's seat. "Warm enough?"

"It's perfect." Regina takes off her gloves and places them on her lap. "Where are we going for dinner?"

"The Outlook."

Her eyes sparkle at the mention of Holly's most scenic restaurant. "Going all fancy, huh?"

"Couldn't afford to in high school, but now . . ." I waggle my eyebrows, trying to pull a laugh from her. When it fills the air, my chest inflates with warmth, as if the sound shot straight to my heart. "There's just something infectious about your laugh." I probably have a goofy expression on my face, but I don't care.

The way her breath catches with the compliment shows me sharing how I truly feel is what matters. I give her a smile, then put the car in drive.

The Outlook overlooks Holly Falls. Though it's dark, we'll be able to see the vastness of the sky from the floor-to-ceiling windows. G loved stargazing in high school. I'm hoping she hasn't changed that much and it's still a favorite of hers.

"Are you ready for the concert tomorrow?" Regina asks.

"Yep. You?"

"Yes. I'm ready to be done with rehearsals."

I laugh. The kids have been all up in our business, and though they don't ask intrusive questions anymore, they watch us like little chicken hawks.

"It's been great hearing you sing again." And if I'm honest, playing piano as she sings feels right..

"It has been great to sing again." She clears her throat. "I, uh, I asked if I could try out for the worship team at church."

"Really?" I glance at her real quick and see her nod. "That's perfect for you."

"You think?"

The hesitancy in her voice tears at me, but I'm more than happy to reassure her. Reaching over, I give her hand a squeeze. "You'll be a fantastic addition."

She lays her palm on top of my hand, and we stay that way until I shift the car into park. Soon we're seated at a table right in front of a window that showcases the drop-off from the bluff, where The Outlook is situated. It's a little unnerving at night, but the way Regina's eyes shine with glee means I'll man up and pretend it doesn't feel like I'm tilting forward.

It's all in your head. The building is stable.

After we order, I look across the table.

Regina meets my gaze, and a soft smile curves her lips. "It's surreal, huh?" she asks.

"Very. It's like my brain is trying to figure out if we should pick up where we left off, which I know logically we can't. But then my brain tries to figure out what this looks like now. Do we get to know each other all over again?"

She nods slowly. "Sort of. I think, unless your favorites have changed, we can skip that."

"Maybe we just skip to the important parts."

"Like what happened between you and Jianna?"

I blink in surprise. She knows my ex-wife's name?

"Is that too much too soon?" Regina asks hesitantly.

"No, no. I was just a little surprised you even knew her name."

"I have a mom who tells me everything. I knew when you got married and when you got divorced."

I stare into her brown eyes. "Did the news affect you any?" I want to punch myself for that dumb question. *Why did I ask that?*

"Honestly? It did. I was surprised by how I felt, but then I reminded myself I got married too. When I heard you were divorced, I felt bad for you and Malea."

"Makes sense. I know my heart broke for you when your mom told me about Max."

Regina shakes her head. "Sometimes it still shocks me that going out for diapers made me a widow. Other times, it seems like that was a lifetime ago."

"What's the hardest part?"

Her eyes tear up. "Knowing he doesn't get to see Kyleigh grow up. He would've loved her so much. Of course, he did the few months he got to see her as a baby. But I mean the girl she is today and whoever she becomes in the future. I hate that he's missing it all." She takes a sip of water. "You?"

"Actually, the same. I hate that Jianna tossed Malea aside for a dream. I don't see why we couldn't have made it work as a team, you know? We could've talked about moving to Nashville or something. But she just woke up one morning and told me she was leaving, and I had absolutely no choice in the matter."

Regina winces. "Shades of me and my dream, huh?"

"Yes, but no. We were teens and terrible communicators. Jianna was my wife. It's entirely different." I pause, gathering the courage I need. "But I do have to ask. Are you here to stay?"

Regina reaches over and threads our fingers together. "I'm not going anywhere."

My shoulders drop, and I realize that niggling fear has been whispering to me this whole time. Knowing G has no plans to leave fills me with sweet relief.

Chapter *twelve*

Theo

Ice skating while in one's mid-thirties is not the brightest idea for a date. Ask me how I know.

I slowly sink down onto the extra cushion I placed on my living room chair. Last night I fell so many times we ended up stopping our skating session early. Instead, we drank hot cocoa and talked until we were too frozen to pay attention to each other. When I dropped Regina off at her house last night, it was with the assurance I'd see her today, because tonight's the Christmas concert at the school.

Our date went really well. Once we cleared the air, the conversation flowed. We caught each other up on the important stuff, promised to communicate ad nauseam, and laughed the night away. I wanted to kiss Regina good-bye, but even though this wasn't technically our first date ever, it was still a first in our new beginning.

I wonder what she's doing this morning.

Grabbing my cell, I open our text thread and send a message.

Theo
Thinking of you.

Before I can set my phone back down, the three dots appear. I lean forward as if I'll actually miss what she's typing.

Regina
You read my mind. Just made a candle that reminds me of you.

Theo
Smells like sweat?

Regina
Smells like a Christmas tree farm and memories.

Okay, why does that make my neck heat and have me wishing I could go straight to her shop and ensure no one buys that candle but me? I'll light it whenever I want to think of G.

I glance around my house and wince. This is obviously a bachelor pad. Brown leather furniture, and besides the Christmas tree, there's no other décor to make the home cozy. I threw all that out when I purged the place after Jianna served me divorce papers. Would Regina actually want to live in a place I tried to make a home with my first wife?

Whoa. Slow down. You've been on one date. You can worry about who moves where once you've dated longer.

But now I'm wondering how many months we have to

date before it's serious enough for me to wonder who lives where. I groan and push the phone away.

"You okay, Dad?"

The sound of my daughter's voice has me shifting until I face her. "Sure am, squirt." I open my arms, and Malea walks straight into them, laying her head against my chest while still standing.

"Ready for school?"

"Do I have to go?" she whines.

"It's the last day before break. You got this."

She lets out a long-suffering sigh. "Fine. But only because today's the Christmas concert."

"I can't wait." And I really can't. Despite all the internal whining I did in the beginning, watching the kids bloom as they grew more confident in their vocals and watching Regina find the love of singing again was worth the late hours I had to work around the farm.

Malea pulls away and studies me. "Did you have a good date?"

Regina and I both told the girls we were going out together. I know for a fact there was a bunch of squealing in both households. Last night we agreed to keep the details to ourselves and just let the girls know we are enjoying our time together.

"I did."

A huge smile splits Malea's face. "Good. My prayers are working."

"You've been praying about this?" My mouth drops. Though why should this shock me? The girls have been plotting a lot this month.

"You teach me how to pray, and then you act shocked I know who God is."

"Smart mouth. Go get your bag so we can go." I smile to let her know I'm not mad.

She giggles and runs out of the room.

"No running."

The day flies by, and soon I'm corralling the kids onto the stage. Everyone's wearing a long-sleeved red t-shirt. G and I both have on red cable-knit sweaters. I'm not even mad we match. In fact, the moment Regina saw my top, she placed a kiss on my cheek.

Matching for the win!

When the kids are all set up, I sit at the piano, and Mr. McCall takes the mic. He's a lot more put together tonight than when he first broke his wrist. He introduces the choir, Regina, and me, then leaves the stage.

Regina and I lock eyes, and I start playing the opening for "Christmas Time Is Here." The kids' voices are angelic, and soon I hear sniffles in the crowd. My own eyes seek Malea's, and the love I have for that child grows. God has blessed me in so many ways, but I'll never stop thanking Him for my precious baby girl. I hate that Jianna is missing this, but it also makes my time with Malea that much more special. No matter what, I'll always be here to cheer Malea on. Whatever plans she makes for her future, she'll have my support. Even if one day she decides to pursue singing professionally. I don't want my fear of abandonment to keep me from championing my little girl.

When the last notes of the last song fill the air, a roar of applause takes its place. The parents stand, giving the kids a standing ovation. The children look giddy with the adoration, and they bow, as we taught them, then silently exit the risers.

Backstage is a cacophony of noise as the kids excitedly

chatter about their performance. The rehearsals paid off. Not a single note was missed.

"Class." Mr. McCall whistles to get everyone's attention. "I'm so proud of you. You were absolutely amazing and brought tears to my eyes." He pretends they're still wet and dabs at the corners of his eyes. The students giggle with delight.

"Please thank Mrs. Parker and Mr. Evers for all of their hard work."

"Thank you," they call out.

"Thank you for letting us help you," Regina says. "We enjoyed it so very much." Her hands are clasped to her chest, and she looks a little misty eyed.

"Are you going to go out now?" Carter asks.

Malea shushes him, but I see Kyleigh give him a slight nod. *Oohs* filter around the room.

"All right, guys, go see your parents and let them praise your talent," the choir teacher says.

"They do that already," Carter announces.

"Then tell them to let some of that air out of the room," Mr. McCall says dryly.

I hide a laugh as Malea, Kyleigh, and Regina walk my way.

"Are we going to celebrate now?" Malea asks.

"How do you usually celebrate?" Kyleigh's brow furrows.

"With a Christmas sundae." I turn to Regina. "Would you two like to join us?"

"Yes, please."

I wrap an arm around Regina and whisper in her ear, "Good, I can't go another minute without being next to you."

"Theo . . ." she whispers.

I pull back, but not before noting the subtle scent she's

wearing. It's new and packs a bigger punch than the one she wore in high school. When I look down, the girls are wearing sappy expressions. Great, are they supposed to love love already? Shouldn't that be something I have to worry about in high school?

But I know they're happy their plan has worked, so I tug on Kyleigh's twists and squeeze Malea's shoulder before guiding them out of the auditorium and into my truck. Time to celebrate like the family I hope we will one day be.

Regina

Who knew a Christmas sundae was actually a thing? The vanilla ice cream has been covered with peppermint sprinkles and hot fudge. There's also a little gingerbread man and Christmas tree cookie sticking out from the concoction. It looks completely decadent but doable considering all four of us are sharing.

I dip my spoon in and sigh with happiness when the flavors hit my tongue. "How did I not know this was a thing?"

"They added it to the menu two years ago. It's great, right?" Theo asks.

I nod while chewing my bite.

"We should make these at home," Kyleigh asks.

"And have a movie night," Malea adds.

"Yes! We need to watch *Polar Express* this time." Kyleigh turns to me. "Can Malea come over again?"

"And me too?" Theo adds with a wink.

Oh my word. Good thing I'm eating ice cream because he's been smoldering at me here and there all night. My sweater already made me warmer than I needed to be so having Theo raise my body temp is making me melt, figuratively and literally. Remembering Theo asked a question, I simply nod assent.

Everything with Theo feels perfect, but also, everything with Theo feels *perfect*. What if it doesn't last? What if we get into a big fight like we did our senior year and break up once again? Or what if he goes out on his farm and a tree falls on him?

As if he can tell I'm spiraling, Theo reaches over and laces our fingers together. The immediate warmth calms the storm within, and I squeeze his hand like the lifeline it is.

Take it one day at a time. Today is good, celebrate. Tomorrow is unknown, leave it alone. The advice my mom gave me centers me, adding to the calm Theo's touch has brought.

The girls start chatting animatedly about some new Christmas movie streaming, and Theo shifts closer. "Did I mention how beautiful you look tonight?"

My cheeks heat. "I'm not wearing anything special."

"Don't you know you make the clothes, not the other way around?"

Okay, charming Theo might be the deadliest version yet. I have no words, but my heart feels like it's growing Grinch style, and I'm not mad at the effect.

"Did I know you were always so charming?" I ask.

"Figured honesty and communicating would work better this time around." He winks, then turns serious. "I was too nervous to tell you how beautiful I thought you were in high school. I didn't want to seem like I was just trying to charm you. This time, I'm not wasting my second chance."

I cover our intertwined fingers with my palm. "Theo, I hope you know I don't consider any time spent with you a waste, whether we end up together or not." It's what I'm trying to remind myself even when I'm tempted to follow the spiraling thoughts.

His Adam's apple bobs. "Does that mean you think there's a chance we won't end up together?"

"More like that's my fear and need to be rational cautioning me."

"I get that. Your life hasn't been easy." His thumb draws circles around the back of my hand.

A lump fills my throat. "Neither has yours." What Jianna did was awful, and I can't help but make the comparison because I know my leaving hurt him as well. Even if he says they're not the same thing, the result was.

"Maybe, but right now, my life feels blessed because you're back in it."

Okay, I need to find a moment alone with this man to give him a kiss that conveys every single emotion going through my heart right now. But because our two chaperones are going gaga over some teen star, I simply squeeze his hand and hope he can read my mind just a little bit.

Judging from the slow smile curving those full lips, Theo has an idea.

When we finish our sundae, the girls throw the mess away as Theo and I come to a stand.

"Will I see you tomorrow?" I ask.

"Definitely. Want to come out to the farm for a movie night? I can get RJ to cover my shift."

"He won't mind?"

"He'd much rather be outdoors than inside."

"I can buy that." RJ was always the first to suggest an outdoor activity when we were younger.

Theo chuckles, and the sound is like a shot of bourbon. Not that I've actually had a shot of bourbon, but if it's what I imagine . . . You know what, never mind. Just take my word, he has the best laugh, the smoothest voice, etc.

Oh, Regina, you are definitely in the sap happy glow of like *like.*

And I am. Being with him is effortless. When my mind isn't trying to think of catastrophes or ways this could go wrong, I'm actually pretty giddy. He texted me first thing this morning and gave me a rose at the Christmas concert, not to mention that precious snowman before our date yesterday.

Theo Evers makes my heart happy, and as long as I can stay in the present, I don't fear a possible future with him.

So stay in the present.

He wraps an arm around my shoulder, and we start a slow gait toward the door. Malea races ahead to get the door and freezes.

"Mom!"

Chapter *thirteen*

Regina

I pace back and forth in my living room as the memory of seeing Jianna Evers earlier this evening assaults my mind.

Why is she here? Does she want Theo back? Is she here merely for Malea?

My eyes squeeze tightly as I remember the joy on Theo's daughter's face. Every little girl needs her mother, and I would never want to stand in the way of that relationship. But I can't help feeling some kind of way. I'm a substitute for the real thing. If Jianna is back for good, then do Theo and Malea even need me? Will Kyleigh and I just be a complication in their lives?

Theo gave me a look that said *Don't pull away*, but my walls were going up before I could even consciously think of how to proceed.

And it's not just my heart I'm worried about. It's all of ours. Mine. Theo's. Kyleigh's. *And* Malea's. I want to believe that Jianna has good intentions and realized what she had right in her own home. The other part fully believes Jianna will wreak havoc this Christmas and not bring peace.

"You gonna tell me why you're mimicking a caged lion?" Kris says wryly.

I stop in my path and stare at my best friend standing in the doorway. Tears well in my eyes as my bottom lip trembles. I can't stop the hurt building in my chest and making its way up my throat.

"Girl . . ." Kris rushes forward and has her arms wrapped around me before the first sob breaks free.

I bury my face in the crook of her neck and let every worry pour out in waterworks. Kris says nothing, merely rubs my back as my body shakes. When I finally calm down, Kris guides us to the sofa.

"What. Happened?" She leans forward, brow furrowed with concern.

"Jianna's back."

Her mouth drops. "The ex?" Her voice raises an octave with the question.

I nod, too spent from crying to say words right now and hoping her volume doesn't wake Kyleigh.

"Why? What does she want? Him? Or just her daughter?"

My breath shudders as she speaks my worries aloud. "I don't know." But I can hear the shakiness in my voice, that *barely holding it together* tone.

"Oh, sweet pea, you aren't thinking this spells tragedy again, are you?"

"What else am I supposed to think?" I throw my hands in the air. "They were married. She's Malea's mother, and that child needs a mother—*wants* a mother—so very much. And now her mother has returned. I can't compete. I *shouldn't* compete." Does it make me a bad person to feel threatened by Jianna's return?

Because all season long, we've been bonding. Sure, Theo and I fought it at first, but we've gotten to bond over music. We've bonded over every single activity the girls signed us up for. Tonight was such a happy, normal moment before Jianna met us coming out of the ice cream shop.

I shouldn't have gotten my hopes up.

"Hey, don't forget she abandoned her family to chase a dream."

I close my eyes. "Am I any better?"

Kris gasps like I just threw Kool-Aid on her favorite pair of white jeans. "You two are *not* the same. I don't know what lies the enemy's got you believing, but you rebuke that and tell him to get behind you stat. You hear me?"

I appreciate what Kris is saying, but how do I explain that I wanted to be on Broadway more than anything? That I ruined one of the best relationships I ever had to chase that fantasy?

"You're not answering me."

"But, Kris—"

She holds up a hand. "But nothing. You were a teenager thinking about her future like *all* teenagers do. You weren't a married woman with a child who decided she didn't like her life and left her obligations."

I wince at the term. How can anyone think of their spouse and child as an obligation? Yet I get what Kris is trying to say. Jianna made promises when she vowed "till death do us part." She became responsible for life when she brought Malea into this world. To toss both aside so cavalierly is appalling.

"Please, G. Please don't think you two are the same. You

went after a possible future like any teen would. You were looking for that next step after high school and planned accordingly. I'm sure however your relationship ended, Theo has forgiven you."

"He said he did." My shoulders relax a little, realizing there might be truth to what Kris is saying.

"Then forgive yourself. You wouldn't hold a grudge against Kyleigh if she decided to pursue singing after high school, would you?"

"No." The word is pulled from my throat with a force that surprises me. "No," I repeat more calmly. "I'd support her."

"As your parents supported you. Then your priorities changed when you married Max. Sounds like Jianna's never did."

Kris is right. I know she is, but I have to get my mind to accept her words as truth. Yes, Theo and I had different visions for our future. No, we didn't talk about it and made assumptions. Yes, I forgive him, and he forgives me.

I'm not like Jianna.

"You're right," I sigh.

"I know." Kris smirks.

A little laugh escapes me. "What do I do now?" My hands twist as I think of what Theo must be facing at this very moment.

"You pray. Pray for Theo, for Malea, and for Jianna." Kris takes in a deep breath and releases it. "She's lost more than Theo and Malea. They'll have to deal with any heartache her presence may bring, but that woman is searching for something to fulfill her. She's the one Jesus would go after."

Oof, the truth hits me, and my knee-jerk reaction of wanting to object is wrong. So I do exactly what Kris says. I bow my head, repent to the Lord, then spend the rest of my night praying for Theo and Malea. For Kyleigh and me. And most importantly, for Jianna.

Only Jesus can make a difference in her life, and I pray that He has the opportunity to do so. I'm not sure if her heart is hardened against religion or what her story is, but I know who the Author and Finisher of faith is. I can only pray she discovers Him as well.

Theo

I never thought I'd see my ex-wife standing in our living room again. Now that she's here, I don't feel any of the feelings I expected. Not heartbreak, not anger for what she's put Malea through. Unfortunately, I don't have any good emotions toward her visit either. My fear is G will withdraw because she thinks I want Jianna back or want to repair our relationship.

And maybe if I thought she came back to Holly for Malea, I'd consider that option. But the way she's eyeing our home and how she has barely said two words to our daughter tells me she has another agenda. Thank goodness I had the sense to send Malea to her room to get ready for bed.

I motion for Jianna to sit across from me, but she takes the cushion next to me, placing her hand on my knee. I slide away, breaking contact, and study her. She looks the same but not. I'm not sure what's different, because it's not hair color or the way she's wearing her makeup, but something has changed.

"Don't be like that." Jianna leans closer.

So I stand up. "What do you want?"

"It's Christmastime. Don't you think it's the perfect time to be a family again?"

I want to laugh, but she seems dead serious. "Jianna, we aren't a family anymore. That broke the day you served me divorce papers. Actually, maybe it broke the day you left without a backward glance toward me *or* our daughter."

"Malea's happy with you, isn't she?"

I think so, but that's not the point. What can I say to this woman that will sink into her thick skull? "You left your daughter six years ago and barely call her. You don't remember her birthday consistently. You essentially forgot her. How do you think that makes her feel?"

"I'm here now, Theo." She huffs. "You're always so self-righteous."

"Asking you to remember Malea isn't self-righteous, Jianna. It's basic parenting. Bare minimum."

"I'm here, aren't I?"

"Yeah, but for how long?"

She shrugs. "Look, I know she's on winter break. I figured you'd be busy with the farm, and I'm happy to help."

I don't believe her, but I'll try to give her the benefit of the doubt. "And when will you return to Nashville?" Because she's evading the question and that makes the hairs on the nape of my neck rise. What is she hiding?

"I think I'm done with Nashville. I haven't made it. I only get gigs here and there but haven't found my big break." Her eyes are downcast.

Part of me sympathizes, and the other part wonders what life would've looked like if she would have simply talked to me. She just made a unilateral decision and left me to pick up the pieces and reassure our daughter it wasn't her fault.

"Where are you staying?" The words come out weary, but I don't have the energy to hide how I really feel.

I'm already tired from this conversation. Plus, I'd rather be talking to Regina and assuring her that I'm all for us. That Jianna being back in Holly doesn't mean the end of the road for us. I can only pray that God will help me get her to see that.

"I thought I could stay here." Jianna blinks up at me innocently.

Yeah, not buying the act. "Pull up your cell and see where you can stay because you can't stay here."

"But this used to be my home," she says, shocked.

"Yeah, *used* to be. We are no longer married, which means you cannot stay here." Honestly, if she were anyone else, I'd offer the guest room. But I don't trust Jianna, and until I know her intentions are from love for Malea, I'm not giving her an inch.

She pouts but finds a place back in town.

"Did you book the B and B?"

"Yes, the one on Main."

Since there's only one in Holly, I didn't need the Main Street qualifier.

"We'll see you tomorrow."

"Can I say good-bye to Malea?" She quirks an eyebrow as if insinuating I'm being ridiculous.

I don't care. I won't have our daughter tossed to the side once again. I'll mitigate any damages I can if possible.

"Fine."

When she walks back into the living room, I stand, ready to see her to the door.

"Can I come over for breakfast tomorrow?" she asks.

"Yeah. Malea will like that."

"Good. I'm sure she's missed me."

I scoff. Is that just now occurring to her? But I don't say anything. I can't. My anger at Jianna's careless attitude toward our daughter is barely contained. Saying something based on my ire and not calm won't do us any good. It never did in the past, and it won't in the present. As long as Jianna is still thinking about Jianna, anything I say will be like talking to a brick wall.

As soon as she leaves, I'm going to the chopping block, and I won't stop until I supply every home in Holly with firewood.

Chapter *fourteen*

Malea

I stare up at the ceiling.

What will today look like? Instead of feeling joy like I always expected when I imagined my mom coming back, I can't forget the look on Mrs. Parker and Kyleigh's faces. They looked shocked. Well, Kyleigh kept looking at me as if trying to figure out how I felt. She knows how much I've wanted my mom around.

The smell of breakfast distracts me, and I slide out of the covers. As I walk down the hall and toward the kitchen, the smell of pancakes and bacon greets me. Dad must have been up for a while already.

He looks up from his cup of coffee and smiles at me. "Morning, squirt."

I try to smile back, but it feels like my lips are too heavy to move upward. And my stomach feels yucky.

"What's wrong?"

I shrug and flop into the dining chair next to Dad.

"Rough night of sleep?" he asks.

"Yeah," I reply softly. I finally know what it means to toss and turn all night.

"Will some pancakes make you feel better?"

"No." But they do smell good. I just don't want to eat them while my stomach is burning with worry.

Dad pulls my chair next to his, and I wince at the screech against the wood.

"Talk to me," Dad pleads. His eyes look all sad.

I don't want him to feel bad, but I don't know how he'll react once I share what I'm thinking. "I feel . . . guilty," I mumble.

He looks surprised. "Why?"

I study my dad, wondering what he'll say if I'm honest. I bite my bottom lip, trying to get the courage to say the truth.

"You can tell me," he says. "I want you to be able to talk to me about anything, no matter what it is." He rubs small circles on my back like he used to do when I was younger.

You can do this, Malea. "I've always wanted Mom to come back and see me. To want to hang out and do the things moms do with their daughters." That's been my prayer since I knew what prayer was.

"Understandable." He looks at me as if he's waiting for me to continue.

"Yesterday, I had that excitement when I first saw her. It was like looking at her was an answer to all my prayers." I pause. This is the tricky part. The part I don't think Dad will like.

He nods for me to keep going.

I drag in a breath and let it all out. "B-but I'm not happy Mom's here. Mrs. Parker looked like she wanted to cry, and

I know Kyleigh was sad they had to leave. I don't want to lose them just because Mom came back. D-does that make me a bad daughter?" And there's the question that kept waking me up at night.

"Baby, no." Dad draws me into a hug.

His hug makes me feel safe, and I burrow closer, wishing that a hug from him would always make everything feel better.

Instead, he pulls back and cups my cheeks, looking me right in the eye. "You could never be a bad daughter. You are fearfully and wonderfully made just like God says you are. Can you make bad decisions? Yes. Is wanting your mother around *and* Regina and Kyleigh a bad thing? No, squirt, not at all."

A tear rolls down my face before I can stop it, but I swipe it away with my hand.

Dad keeps staring at me, love shining in his eyes. "You love your mom, Kyleigh, and Regina, and that speaks to how big your heart is. God made your heart that way, and it's one of the reasons I love you so much. You show me how it looks when someone listens to God and loves Him and others."

"I do?" My voice feels shaky, but this makes me feel so much better. I *do* love Mom and Kyleigh and Mrs. Parker. Maybe I don't have to choose one person over the other, and I can love them all.

"Yes! You teach me so much every day. I mean, you even wanted to teach me how to flirt."

I giggle as Dad makes a funny face.

"Please don't ever think you're bad, okay?"

"Okay."

"And don't feel guilty for wanting to love as many people

as you can, 'kay? That's God's work right there, and I'm proud of you."

"Thanks, Daddy."

I hug him again because he gives the best hugs. He kisses the top of my head, and I want to cry again, but this time happy tears.

"You know you're the best thing that ever happened to me, right?" he whispers.

"You've said that before," I mumble against his shirt. Yet every time I hear it, it makes my heart feel like it's filling up my chest. Can a heart grow from hearing something like that?

"But do you believe it?" Dad asks seriously, pulling away once again to look me in the eye.

He always does this when he wants me to know what he's saying is important. So I try to copy his look and stare straight at him as well.

"Yes. You've always been here. Even when you're grumpy or out chopping wood, you still tell me how much you love me."

"Because I do. You're a gift from God that I never want to take for granted. When we read from the book of Luke and Mary finds out she's going to have a child, I always think about when your mom found out she was pregnant. I've never felt such joy. Please don't ever think any different." He squeezes my hand.

But his statement makes me think of one of my fears. "What about Mom? Do you think she regrets having me?"

He pauses, and I see his Adam's apple move up and down as if he doesn't know what to say.

Finally, Dad speaks. "What do you think God would say about that?"

My brow wrinkles as I think about some of the things they say in Sunday school. And what Dad is always saying. "Um, He would say I'm fearfully and wonderfully made?"

Dad smiles like he's proud. "Exactly."

"Does that mean it doesn't matter how Mom feels about me? Only how God feels?"

Dad's eyes look watery. "I think that's exactly what it means. Even me"—he points to his chest—"you know how much I love you, but what matters more?"

"How much God loves me?"

Dad leans down and kisses me on the top of my head. "Exactly, squirt. I love you more than I can say, but God loves you enough that He sent Jesus to earth for you."

That's right. That's why Jesus was born. That's why Jesus died for me, for Dad, *and* for Mom. I'm not sure what will happen or how long my mom will be here, but I have to trust that God loves me.

Theo

I get out of my truck and look left, right, then left again before crossing the street. Now the shop is in my sights, and I'm not taking my eyes off Scents and Sensibility for nothing. A quick glance inside shows only one customer, which means I'm automatically next in line the moment I cross the threshold. I'm so thankful that RJ agreed to watch Malea so I could come talk to Regina.

The second I open the door a fragrance that smells a lot like my tree farm greets me. My lips quirk at the thought that this might be the candle Regina made with me in mind.

Her gaze flits to mine and freezes, then returns to the customer at her register.

Since she's busy, I decide to meander around the shop and take in the many offerings she has. I incorrectly assumed Regina had candles in a jar and that was all. That idea is so simplistic compared to what she actually sells. There are Christmas tree–shaped candles, others shaped like snowmen and candy canes. There are also wax melts, diffusers, and those little sachet things my mom used to put in our dresser drawers.

When I get near the back of the shop, I even spy some air fresheners. Pride blooms in my chest at all she's accomplished. Maybe this is how Regina felt when she came to the tree farm. The night she and Kyleigh made wreaths, G looked in awe of my accomplishments. All I saw was the hard work that went into running the place. Not that the farm is a burden, I love it, but it *is* hard work.

The door chimes as the customer leaves, and I turn to face Regina, who's still standing at the register.

"Hi." I lift my hand in a casual wave and immediately feel like an idiot for doing so. So not smooth.

"Hey." She glances outside and sees no one coming.

The next instance she's in front of me, arms wrapped around my waist. My breath swooshes out in relief as I pull her close to me.

Regina tilts her head back and looks up at me. "I've been praying for you."

"Yeah?" I tuck a strand of her hair behind her ear.

She nods. "Are you okay? Malea?" She pauses a beat. "Jianna?"

I glance around her space. "Can we sit? Do you have a moment to talk?"

"Until the next person walks in." She slides her hand in mine. "Follow me."

Happily. I don't say anything until we're at a table in the back room. She offers me a water, but I decline. I don't want to get distracted from this conversation.

"So . . ." Regina prompts.

I run a hand down my face. "Jianna followed us home last night to talk. She did *not* stay at my place."

"Theo." Regina reaches over to stop me. "Even if she did, I wouldn't have questioned it because I know who you are."

I interlace our fingers. "Thank you for saying that. But I also don't want there to be any misconceptions. She stayed at the B and B." I didn't even flinch when she arrived to have breakfast with Malea after our heart-to-heart.

"Okay. Continue."

"Yeah, so we talked. She claims she's giving up on making it in Nashville. That she knew Malea's winter break would be happening and decided to come see her."

"How's Malea?"

I tell her about the conversation we had this morning.

"Oh man." She places a hand against her heart. "That poor baby. I hope you squeezed her tight and said how much she's loved."

"You know it." I smile, loving how in sync we are.

Regina sags into her chair. "Good." She tilts her head. "What next?"

And here's where it gets dicey. I'm hoping what I have to share will land correctly and G won't question where my heart is, but I also don't know.

"We go skiing."

"Huh?" Her brows raise.

The look is so adorable I'm sure there's a mushy expression on my face. "Every year since Malea was born, we've gone skiing the weekend before Christmas. There's a resort we go to near Tahoe City. It's usually just a couple of days because I can't be away from the farm that long."

"Jianna is going to go skiing with you and Malea?" Regina folds her arms across her chest as if protecting herself from the news.

"She brought it up this morning in front of Malea. Since it's tradition, I said yes." I watch Regina's face for any clues she's unhappy. "Say something, G."

She reaches out to squeeze my hand. "Don't worry about me. Do what's best for Malea, for you, and even for Jianna."

I want her to truly mean that, but I'm terrified this whole business will push the best woman I ever knew away. "Are you sure?" I ask pointedly.

"Of course I am. Do I like that your ex-wife is back? No. Do I want Malea to be able to spend time with her? All the yeses."

"Thank you." Some of the tension seeps out of my shoulders, but honestly, I won't feel better until Jianna's intentions are clear. "Oh, and one more thing."

"What's that?"

"Malea wants to know if Kyleigh can come with us. She's so excited about having a best friend and wants to share the experience with her. But also, she's afraid of losing Kyleigh's friendship."

"She has nothing to worry about. Malea is all Kyleigh talks about these days. Her and Kris." Regina smiles. "I'll tell her about the trip."

I hesitate, then ask what's on my heart. "Would you go too?"

"Me?" Her eyes widen. "I don't think that's a good idea.

Jianna's there to spend time with Malea, and sometimes women are territorial if there's another person involved in their kid's life. I don't want to mess anything up for Malea."

I cup Regina's face and rub my thumb across her smooth skin. "How did I get so lucky to get another chance with you?"

"Theo . . ." she murmurs, lashes fluttering against her cheek.

It feels like an invitation to close the gap. I inch forward, then stop. I've gone ninety percent, but I need to know Regina wants this kiss as much as I do.

Her eyes open in question, and she stares straight into mine before they close once more, and the gap evaporates.

Chapter *fifteen*

Regina

Kissing Theo is like coming home. He snakes an arm around my waist, tugging me closer, while his other hand cups the back of my head. He's all in, like he's treasuring every single part of this moment. My body's aglow, as if I just sat in front of my fireplace with a cup of cocoa.

But kissing my ex, who is now my new beginning, is better than any cup of cocoa I could ever concoct. My heart races with each press of his lips.

The door chimes, and I jolt in his arms, coming to my senses. We're in Scents and Sensibility, a public place. Thank goodness no one can see into the back room from the front.

Theo caresses my cheek before pulling away completely. "I'll see you later?" he asks, voice all husky.

A shiver racks my frame, and I want to lean right back into his arms. Judging by his knowing grin, he knows exactly where my thoughts went. He leans forward and presses a soft kiss right below my jaw, then stands up.

"Later, G." He winks and is gone before my brain can catch up to my eyesight.

I press a hand to my hair, assuring all my strands are where they should be. There's nothing I can do about the just-kissed look, but I can at least dispel any rumors by tidying up my hair. I head toward the front with a smile on my face and pause when I see Kris.

"So"—she hooks a thumb over her shoulder—"is my imagination accurate? Or did you just *talk*?" There's a twinkle in her eye that shows she knows how much she's getting under my skin.

I pick up the nearest potpourri sachet and toss it at her. "Hush."

Kris cackles, hands crossing her waist as she bends over. She stands up and wipes the tears from her eyes. "I hope that was a good first kiss."

My lips automatically curve into a smile before I can keep my cards close to my vest.

"Oh wow. That good, huh?"

"I'm not the kind of woman who kisses and tells."

"You don't have to, girl. Your face is saying it all."

I shake my head, then turn away because my cheeks are heating up like the Fourth of July. It's like I'm the Human Torch, and my whole body is aflame. Who knew Theo could outdo my memories of our time together?

"Did you two get everything straightened out?" Kris asks.

"Sort of. He's taking into consideration what Malea needs, navigating the waters with Jianna, and making sure I'm not threatened by all of it. He's definitely juggling a lot right now." I stare at my friend. "And he's planning on taking the girls and his ex skiing."

Kris's mouth drops. "Wow. Is he a glutton for punishment?"

"It's a tradition."

"At least it's not camping," she says with a chuckle.

My brow furrows, thinking back to the whole *Parent Trap* business the girls tried to pull off. "I don't really think the girls would try and chase Malea's mom off. Besides, she's not the evil stepmother wannabe." *Yikes*. "Wait, in this case, am *I* the evil stepmom?"

"No way. Again, you didn't abandon your child."

I wave my hand in the air. "You're right, but also, I can't see Malea doing something like that. She's such a sweet child." I tilt my head and study Kris. "Enough about me. What are you up to?"

She's wearing slacks and a nice blouse. Her trench coat is open, giving her a business-casual look. I can't remember the last time I saw her this dressed up.

"Had an interview."

"Where?"

"At Time of Knead."

I frown. "But your degree is in kinesiology."

Kris rubs the middle of her forehead. "I know, but I need a job, G. At this point, anything will do."

That's not true. If God is shaking things up for Kris, then where she gets a job matters because it's part of His greater plan. Guess it's my turn to pour some wisdom into her.

"Have you prayed about what to do next?"

"I really don't like when things flip in our relationship." She glowers at me.

I smirk. "Ha. You can dish it out but can't take it."

"I mean, I told God I needed a job." She winces, as if hearing her words for the first time.

"Oh yeah, I bet that made a whole difference in your job search."

"I *did* have an interview."

I cross my arms. "Did she offer you a job?"

"No," Kris mumbles.

"Might be because you have a kinesiology degree," I reiterate. "Girl, stop messing around and ask what God wants for you."

"What if I can't hear Him?"

I pause for a moment, trying to hear the nuances of what she's *not* saying. Because Kris has to be one of the most prophetic people I've ever met. You know how the Israelites told Moses to keep on talking to God, but they would just hang back? Yeah, that's how I feel being around Kris sometimes. It's *obvious* God talks to her, and she always listens and is obedient to what He says. So her stressing about not hearing Him tells me something else is going on.

"Why would you worry about that?" I ask cautiously.

She swallows and looks away. "I can't hear Him anymore."

"You think you can't or genuinely can't?"

She blows out a breath. "Both?"

Hmm. "What have you done differently?"

"I might have gotten mad at Him." She folds her arms around her waist. "I mean. Neil left. I can't have children. And when you moved out, I felt alone."

My mouth drops, but she holds up a hand.

"I'm not blaming you. I'm just saying I've been in this funk for years now. Seeing my ex-husband move back with a family finally shook me out of my stupor." She plays with the belt of her jacket. "But it was also the first time in a while that I heard God when He told me to move. It was just so obvious, so I did."

"Then trust that. He spoke to you. He's not a God who abandons us."

"I know you're right, but . . ."

"But you're still worried?"

She nods.

I walk to her and hold out a hand. "Then let's pray together." This girl has been through many ups and downs, and I'm all too happy to stand by her and support her through one of her downs.

Kyleigh

I'm going on a ski trip. Ever since Malea invited me to join her and her dad I've been so happy. I've never been on a father-daughter trip, and though Malea's mom is going too, I still have hope that my mom and Malea's dad will be the ones singing happily ever after when it's all over.

I pull the photo frame that has the picture of me and my dad in it and stare. I'm only a baby in the picture, so I can't see any resemblance between us. That's not why it's one of my favorite pictures. It's my dad's smile that always makes me feel better. He looks so happy, like nothing else could be better than holding me.

Mom always reminds me that Dad loved me so much and would love who I am today just as much. And looking at this picture, I can believe it. Hopefully Dad understands that I want to experience that kind of love from a father now too. I know that Malea's dad isn't my father, but going on this trip feels like an opportunity to get what I've always wanted.

I don't usually tell Mom how often I think about having a dad. Hers is still around, so she doesn't really get it. But I wonder about the expression *daddy's girl* and wonder what else I'm missing out on since my dad isn't alive anymore.

"Kyleigh, Malea's here," Mom calls.

I place the frame back on my nightstand and race down the hall, slowing when I get near the end of the hallway. I don't want Mom yelling for me to slow down or keep me from going out with Malea and Mr. Evers. We're going supply shopping for our trip, and I'm so excited. This is the first time it'll be just me, Malea, and her dad.

Malea and Mr. Evers are waiting at the door.

"You ready?" Mr. Evers asks.

I nod.

"You sure you don't want to come, G?" he asks Mom.

Mom places a kiss on his cheek, and Malea and I stare at each other in glee. Our plan is working. They've been on a date, and now they've kissed each other. Sure, it doesn't look like the kisses at the end of the Hallmark movies, but this is definitely moving in the right direction. We do our handshake and then muffle our giggles under our hands.

But then Mr. Evers is calling for us to leave, and Mom is telling me to have fun.

"See you later." I wave to Mom.

"Bye, Kyleigh Bear."

I sit in the back seat with Malea, and we chat the whole way to the store. It's weird not seeing her in school every day, but I'm so glad that we're on winter break. I'd rather every day be winter break so I can experience the magic of Christmas versus sitting in a classroom all day with smelly boys.

Mr. Evers pulls up to the ski shop on Main Street and parks his truck. It's not a red truck like you see on Christmas pillows. Instead, it's blue and newer looking.

"Mr. Evers?"

"Theo." He smiles at me, so I smile back.

"Theo, why isn't your truck red? You own a Christmas tree farm."

He laughs as we cross the street. "Because those kind of trucks are a classic. I can't afford one."

"Then why didn't you buy a newer red truck? How can you have a tree farm without a red truck?"

"You love all things Christmas, huh?"

I nod.

"How about this? I'll paint my truck for you."

My mouth drops. "Really? You'd do that for me?" I point at my chest to make sure he knows it's me and not Malea asking.

Malea stands by me as if she realizes how important this is to me.

"I'd be happy to. But it might not happen until next Christmas. Is that okay?"

I nod my head until I get a little dizzy.

He chuckles. "Okay. Until then, we can always Rudolph the truck."

"What does that mean?" Malea and I ask at the same time.

"It means we buy reindeer ears and a red nose to place on the vehicle. We'll do it after we get our gear."

Malea and I high-five each other and then we're off. Mr. Evers—Theo—brought a list with him. We get a ski jacket and pants for me. Mr. Evers said we can rent skis at the resort, so I don't have to worry about owning my own pair. We also get clothing that Theo calls a base layer.

I've never been shopping with a dad before. Even Grandpa hasn't taken me shopping. When we're done, we go to another store, and Theo buys the items so we can Rudolph his truck. By the time we get to the truck, Malea and I are giggling, and it actually feels like we're a family. Theo lets me place an antler on one side of the truck while Malea does it to the other. Then he places the nose on the front of the truck.

"This is the best," I say.

"How about I take a picture?" Theo asks.

"Yes!" Malea grins.

We sit on top of the front hood, and he tells us to smile.

"I'll send this to your mom so you can have a copy, Kyleigh."

"Thanks, Theo."

I'm not sure what's going to happen between him and Mom, but I hope they stay together forever.

When we get in the back seat, Malea leans over to me. "You have got to get your mom to come skiing with us."

I nod. I was thinking that already, but now we can plan a way to make it happen together.

Chapter *sixteen*

Regina

"Are you really not going skiing with us?" Kyleigh grouses.

I smirk at my persnickety ten-year-old. She's been acting like a bear, stomping around the house because I won't budge about staying home. "That's right. Malea needs some bonding time with her mother. I'll just be in the way."

"What about me? I won't get bonding time with *my* mother."

"No, but you will get to hang out with Theo some more. Weren't you the one telling me how much you needed a father figure in your life? He'll teach you all about skiing, and you get to go with your best friend."

"No, no, no." She wags a finger in the air. "I wanted a family with you, Malea, her dad, and me. Not Malea's mom."

I stifle a chuckle. "Don't you want Malea to be happy?"

"Mom!" Kyleigh whines at a decibel that'll have our neighbor's dog barking any moment. "Don't you know I just need to whine."

"Oh, my bad, ma'am." I place a hand on my hip, staring at my child who thinks she's grown.

"And puh-lease don't *ma'am* me. I'm younger than you."

"Ouch. Because I'm so ancient."

"You *were* born last century."

No one tells you that the most daggers thrown at you in life are from your own offspring. The more this child of mine picks at my age, the older I feel, and the more I'm assured God gave parents children to stay humble.

"Kyleigh Ann Parker, poke that lip back in and go get ready for movie night."

"Fine." She slinks out of the living room.

They'll leave for the ski resort on Friday, and she's bent on getting me to join them. But I know how much Theo is struggling with Jianna being around. So far she's eaten dinner with them every night this week. A whole three days that feels like a lifetime.

The doorbell rings, and I blink. Theo and Malea are a whole hour early, but that's not actually a bad thing. I miss Theo. Texts just aren't the same as seeing him in person, but the Christmas tree farm has been busier as Christmas draws closer.

I toss my throw blanket aside and pad to the door. But when I open it, Theo and Malea aren't waiting on the other side. Jianna is. I glance over my shoulder to ensure Kyleigh's not in sight. Though she may come back out of her room again. I grab a jacket from the coat rack and slip it on, closing the door behind me.

Jianna steps back and frowns. "You're not going to invite me in?"

"I'm not sure I want my daughter to hear our conversation."

Jianna nods slowly. "Fair enough."

I motion to the chairs on my front porch. "Should we sit?"

"Yes." Her breath puffs between us.

We sit and silence descends. My insides are twitchy as I wait for her to start speaking. Is she here to start trouble or actually here for maturity's sake?

"I've heard a lot about you from Malea these past few days." The words are innocent, but the tone behind them isn't.

My stomach clenches. "Oh?" Hopefully my tone is curious and nonthreatening.

"I know who you are."

I meet her stare. *I have nothing to apologize for.* The phrase repeats in my head a few times before Jianna speaks again.

"I think you should stick to your house, your side of town, and leave my family alone."

Lord God . . . The words come out in a prayer because the other part of me—the *flesh* part of me—wants to come out of this chair. *Who does she think she is? She can't waltz back here and demand I stay away from Theo.*

Holy Spirit, please empower me to act in love and not the way that miniature devil on my shoulder is egging me on.

But she is *Malea's mom and Theo's ex-wife. What if they have a chance to reconcile? Who am I to stand in the way?*

The last thought cools the fire raging in me. Doesn't the Bible talk about husbands and wives being reconciled to each other, even exes? The fight leaves me, and I try my best not to shrink back.

"You do know my daughter is best friends with yours, right?" Kyleigh would be crushed if I tell her not to talk to Malea anymore.

"Is Malea the only child in Holly? She can make other friends."

"I didn't say Malea was her only friend but that she's her *best* friend. Don't you want what's best for your daughter?" I stare at the woman who hurt those I care for.

"Are you saying I'm not looking out for her interest?" She sucks her teeth. "She's *my* child. I carried her for nine months. I think I know what's best for her."

Yet she hasn't been around for the last six years. I keep that comment from exiting my mouth, but just barely. This seems like a situation that doesn't have a good ending.

"Look." She blinks rapidly, and I have to try not to laugh at how her lashes remind me of a caterpillar. "Your daughter can come on the ski trip, but then I don't want to see her again. Your interference in my marriage isn't appreciated." Jianna stands up and looks down on me.

I mean, *really* looks down on me. Though I don't want this woman to come to my home and make me feel like I've sinned, that's exactly what she's succeeded in doing. My mouth dries as I stand on my own two feet, trying to find my spine of steel instead of grappling with the feeling of getting sucker punched with kryptonite.

"Once she's back from the ski trip, you keep her away from Malea, and you sure as well better stay away from my husband." She whirls away with that last parting remark and stalks down the sidewalk toward a sports car waiting by the curb.

What just happened?

I walk back inside and sink onto the sofa cushion as if I'm in a daze. Strangely, part of me is relieved. I *knew* having Jianna Evers back in Holly was going to mean tragedy for me. The warring in my mind of the whole *will it* or *won't it* is finally over. It's definitely a yes. I no longer have to wonder. But the other part of me . . . The other part of me wants to curl into a ball and sob.

Don't give in. It's the Christmas season. Your daughter is healthy. Kris is turning a corner.

As for me, God has me in the palm of His hand. If that means that my relationship with Theo is coming to an end so that he can make amends with his wife, then so be it. For a sweet moment, I got to feel those sparks of interest. To remember what it's like to yearn for another person.

Now I have the opportunity to put someone else's happiness above my own. I've discovered I can let my heart feel again and not fall apart. If all this relationship becomes is a stepping stone to something else, then I'll hold these memories close until they no longer serve a purpose.

The only question in my mind now is, How do I break up with Theo once again?

Theo

Something's wrong with Regina. Ever since Malea and I arrived, she's been giving me a wide birth. She flinched when I greeted her with a kiss to the cheek. And I swear, every time Jianna's mentioned, she pales. Of course it's a little hard to see if color is actually leaching out of her brown face, but it *appears* that way.

The girls are enthralled with the movie and make comments here and there, preventing me from asking G what's up. Instead, I'm forced to try to concentrate on the film when the person who really has my attention is at the other end of the couch, our girls between us as buffers.

Malea and Kyleigh laugh in unison, and I glance over at Regina just in time to see her look away. *Ugh!* I want to shake something, but more importantly, I want her to tell me what's wrong. I'm not naïve, there's something weighing heavily on her mind.

My throat dries. Is she going to break up with me?

That can't be it, can it? Up until now, we've been good. Exchanging text messages all day every day. After our kiss at the candle shop the other day, I thought for sure we were right as rain. We even talked about the future a little bit. I'd been over the moon that Regina was willing to consider a future with me. I know how much she wants to avoid hurt, which is why this whole one-eighty is messing with my mind.

What did I do? Was it something I said? *Didn't* say?

Focus on the movie. You won't find out what it is until you can talk to her alone.

Unfortunately, that advice is useless. I struggle through every second of the film until the credits roll, and the girls run off to Kyleigh's room. As soon as I hear the door close, I scoot a cushion closer to Regina and take her hands in mine.

"What happened?"

She swallows audibly, and her gaze flits away.

My heart sinks. This isn't good. "G?" I ask softly. But I'm not going to beg. Been there and finally healing from the scars. No need to open those wounds back up again.

"Jianna came to see me." She meets my gaze, and her brown eyes are full of worry.

"What did she say?"

"Nothing good."

I close my eyes but open them back up quickly. If Regina

is going to do what I think she's going to do, I'd rather her rip off the bandage than this slow pull.

"Theo . . ."

I brace myself.

"She wants you back."

I scoff. "No, she doesn't. She wants what she can't have. I was too foolish to see it when we first got married, but fortunately, I wised up. Whatever she said to you, don't believe her."

Regina's eyes dart left and right as if studying every single thing in my gaze. "Do you want to reconcile with her?"

"What?" I jerk back. "No. She *abandoned* us, G."

"I know." Her eyes well up. "But, biblically speaking, don't you have a duty to try and reconcile if she truly wants that?"

I want to run away from this conversation, find Jianna, and demand she fix this. Because something tells me that Regina doesn't want to believe me. That she wants to find a reason not to be together. But maybe that's me falling into Jianna's trap. I take a moment to pray for wisdom before speaking.

"If we were separated, then, yeah, I believe reconciliation should be attempted. It's what I attempted and asked for, but she willingly abandoned us and happily sent divorce papers. She refused to go to counseling or stay married while attempting a singing career. At one point, she was living with another man in Nashville. I haven't figured out her angle, but I don't believe a single word out of her mouth." I drag in a breath, trying to calm my racing heart. "I hate to say this, but I don't think trying to reconcile with a person who is acting in that manner is good for me or Malea. So, no, I don't think I have to reconcile with her."

Regina drops my hands and pulls the throw blanket around her body. The space between us widens acutely and feels like a stab to the heart. But I have to remember the hurt she's been through, how easily Jianna lies, and pray that God can sort through it all.

"What do you want to do?" I finally ask.

"I need to pray. To think about all of this."

"Fair."

Her gaze searches mine. "You're okay with that?"

"I'll never discourage you from talking to God about something. If anything, in this situation, I *want* that. Because if you won't believe me, maybe you'll believe Him."

"It's not that I don't believe you. It's that I don't trust the situation. I don't trust that I won't get hurt somehow. It seems like that's the guarantee in my life—pain."

"Then I'll go and let you have the space to pray and hear from God." I clear my throat. "Can I pray for you before I go?"

Regina's head bobs up and down quickly. "Please," she croaks.

"Father God, I pray that You give G all the wisdom she needs. This is a sticky situation. She's getting conflicting information, and I can only imagine how that feels." Aw, man, I really do get it. She's gotta be feeling weary by this all. "Please bring clarity and peace to us all through this. In Jesus's name, amen."

G wraps me in a hug that's over before I can even react. "Thank you."

"Call me when you want to talk, 'kay?" I hold in a sigh.

She nods.

I call Malea, and we say good-bye. I say nothing on the way back home, but thankfully, Malea chatters away happily, sensing nothing wrong. I hope that when Regina's done praying and sitting on this situation with God, we can pick off where we left off. Happy and on the way to falling in love.

Please help her see I'm telling the truth.

Chapter *seventeen*

Theo

The whack of my ax echoes in the clearing near my house. I've been chopping wood all morning, and I've certainly got enough to add to the lot for sale. Still, I don't feel any better than when I first came out here. The fact that my ex-wife is trying to ruin my chance at a good future has me chopping so much wood my shirt is soaked through. It's just so infuriating that she keeps playing these games, and I'm helpless to watch as she hurts me and those I care about.

"All right, man. That's enough."

I look over my shoulder. RJ leans against a tree, watching me with concern.

"You're soaked through. You trying to get sick?"

"You're not my father." Who cares if I just had the same thought.

"No, but I am your friend. You passed healthy outlet a couple of hours ago, I'd imagine." RJ scans the ground and the wood lying about. He points toward the house. "Go change and I'll gather this into bundles."

I rub the back of my neck. "You don't have to do that."

"Theo, just listen."

I stick the ax into the chopping block, then head inside. Once inside, I realize how disgusting I really am. A quick shower, dry clothes, and I'm back outside to help RJ. My ax is gone, which means he probably stored it in the nearby shed. Half the wood has made a disappearance as well. I bend over and start to gather the rest.

"'Bout time you came back out." RJ smirks. "Took a shower?"

"I was sweaty."

"Gee, I wonder how that happened." RJ shakes his head as he gathers up wood. "What crawled up your backside?"

"Jianna told Regina she wants me back and basically tried to warn her off."

RJ lets out a low whistle. "That's some shady . . ." His voice trails off. "What are you going to do? Other than supply the whole county with firewood."

"Hey, there's snow in the forecast next week."

"Yeah, well, now we don't have to worry about freezing." RJ ties rope around his bundle. "Seriously, bro, what are you going to do?"

I shrug. "Let God sort it all out."

"You're not worried Regina's going to step back? Create distance?" RJ winces.

"I mean, she kind of already has. She barely looked at me last night. Before I left, she admitted she didn't want to get hurt. Not that I blame her." Still, I wanted to say, *What about me?* I don't want to get hurt either.

Then again, I'm not sure how abandonment compares with widowhood.

They're incomparable. Hurt is hurt.

"Have you talked to Jianna?"

I blow out a breath. "She's coming over tomorrow to have breakfast with Malea. I'll talk to her then."

"Good luck." RJ grimaces.

"You don't think that's a good idea?"

"It's not that." He runs a hand down his beard. "Honestly, that woman is up to something."

"You think?" Sarcasm drips from every syllable. I may have been slow to notice her conniving ways when we were married, but I won't be fooled twice.

"Good thing I'm going with you on the ski trip."

He's right. There's no way I want to be alone with Jianna, even if Malea *and* Kyleigh will be there. Honestly, I wish G would come too, but I admire how she doesn't want to get in the way of Jianna's mother-daughter bond. There isn't one, but maybe that's the whole point.

"I'll make sure she doesn't try anything."

I instantly deflate and realize how tense I've been since my ex-wife returned to Holly. "You have no idea how much I appreciate it."

"Enough to lay off the chopping block for a while?"

I huff. "Yeah, I'll do that."

RJ slaps my back so hard I think my soul momentarily leaps from my body. He chuckles like he knew exactly what he did.

"See ya?"

I nod. "Later."

That night, I toss and turn until the sun rises once again, and I find myself in the kitchen making breakfast. Malea walks in, rubbing sleep from her eyes. She gives me a quick hug, then slinks into a chair, laying her head on the table.

"Tired, squirt?"

"Mm-hmm."

"Well, your mom should be here any minute."

I hear a noise and glance over my shoulder to see Malea prop herself up by the elbow. "Dad?"

"Yeah?"

I wince as bacon grease pops me. Guess I should pay attention to the food.

"Do you think Mom will move back to Holly?"

My stomach drops to my toes. Jianna back in Holly full-time? I want to laugh at the ridiculous notion, but I know it's probably a hope and a dream for my daughter.

"I'm not sure, Malea."

"Do you think I can ask her when she gets here?"

I want to say no in order to protect her heart, but also, maybe Jianna will surprise us all. "Do you want me to do it instead? I can ask her when you're not around in case the answer isn't what you want to hear."

Quiet descends, and I give her the space to process as I pray that Jianna really does surprise me. I don't want my daughter hurt. It took her a while to stop crying for her mom when she was younger. Even now, Malea still keeps looking for Jianna to show up.

"Yeah, that sounds like a better idea."

I walk over and place a kiss on her forehead. "Done."

The bell rings, and she pops up with a quickness. "I'll get it."

"Don't forget to check the peephole first."

"I know, I know," she mutters as she races toward the front of the house.

The sound of Jianna's voice is muffled but unfortunately confirms her presence here. It took me a while to feel like this place was mine and Malea's and contained no more traces of her. Now I might have to redecorate when she vanishes once again—okay, I'm leaning more toward seventy-five percent sure she's not sticking around in Holly, not one hundred.

"Something smells good."

My shoulders are around my ears the minute I hear her voice.

I place plates on the table. "I'll let you two eat, and then I'll come back later. Wanted to chat about something," I say, finally looking my ex in the eyes.

An alluring smile curves her lips—at least, that's what she's attempting, but the expression only turns my stomach. "Why don't we talk now?"

I glance at Malea, who nods. "Fine."

Malea grabs her breakfast and points down the hall. I nod, and she leaves so I take her empty chair.

"What do you want to talk about?" Jianna leans forward, her lips pursed. I don't know if she thinks that's sexy, but all I see is the woman who left her family.

Also, she hasn't tried to flirt since she first got here and I told her no. Now all of a sudden she's trying again? I can't help thinking it ties into her meeting with Regina.

"Are you moving back to Holly?" I ask point-blank.

She rears back. "What on earth would make you think that?"

Aha! "Then you're not?"

"I didn't say that either." She leans forward again, tracing a finger down my arm.

I move my arm. "We're not married, so don't touch me."

"Theo," she whines. "Don't be like that."

"I'm in a relationship with someone else."

Her lip curls. "Is she still talking to you? Because I'm pretty sure I made myself clear." She stops, eyes widening at what she let slip.

"Oh, I heard. I also set her straight, because me and you"—I point back and forth between us—"we're not a thing."

"We could be if she weren't in the way."

I scoff. "No. The only thing that could earn you a second chance is if God talked from the heavens like He talked to Hosea and told me to remarry again."

Her countenance darkens. "Are you calling me a . . . ?" She swallows. "We aren't married. I can be with whomever I want."

"Pretty sure you should only be with the person you're married to." But her answer confirms what I thought. She's already moved on.

"Whatever." She rolls her eyes. "Your ideals are so antiquated."

She's not wrong. My ideas go back to the beginning of time. I should've known Jianna wasn't the one for me when I had the slightest inkling she didn't value a relationship with God like I do. Scratch that, *have* a relationship with God like I do.

"Why are you here, Jianna?" My question gives away the weariness in my soul, but I gotta know. I can't tiptoe around this subject anymore.

"To see Malea."

"Really? That's it?"

She shrugs.

"Yeah, I'm not buying it. Are you moving back so you can see her? Will you make plans for next week?"

She flinches.

Thought so. "You want to spend time with her on Christmas? New Year's?"

"Look," she interrupts me. "Let me just be honest."

Finally!

"I need some cash." She licks her lips. "My ex kicked me out, and I had no other place to go. I thought I'd kill two birds by seeing Malea for a little bit and making some money."

"How do you plan on making money? You don't have a job here."

"Well, you weren't happy to see me and made sure I knew we were never getting back together." She shakes her head. "So I tried another tactic."

"Regina."

She nods. "Look, just give me some cash to tide me over, and I'll leave your first love alone."

"And will you come back?"

"Malea's doing just fine with you."

So no.

Money. That's what it always boils down to. Still, my heart hurts for Malea. She's been looking forward to having her mom around. How can I tell her she was a mere afterthought?

Malea

She doesn't want me.

Why? What did I do?

I want to run back into the kitchen and get answers, but I probably won't like what else Mom has to say any more than I do now. I'm glad Dad's having this conversation because I don't want her to see me cry. She's not worth my tears.

I grip my plate and finally go to my room. The idea of seeing Mom again, spending any time with her, makes me sick to my stomach. I'm not sure how I'm supposed to eat my breakfast now. But if I don't, then Dad will know I heard the conversation. Eavesdropping is a big no-no with him.

What do I do?

I grab my cell and dial Kyleigh's number. She'll give me advice, or maybe I can even talk to her mom. Would Mrs. Parker want to talk to me after whatever Mom did? More tears leak, and I hate the break in my voice when my BFF answers.

"What's wrong?" Kyleigh asks.

I sniffle some more. "My mom doesn't like me."

"What happened?"

I tell her everything I heard.

"Lele, I'm so sorry. What can I do?"

"I don't know. Do you think your mom knows what to do?"

"Let's ask her. Just a second."

I hear nothing for a couple of minutes, then the kindest voice comes across the speaker.

"Malea, are you okay?"

Tears pour down my face. "No." I sniffle, trying to control myself.

"Kyleigh told me what happened. Sweetie, I can't imagine how much this hurts, but please know that you are loved. I know how much your dad loves you. And I hope it's okay to say, but I love you too."

I cover my mouth so Dad and Mom can't hear me crying. But these tears aren't the ones ripping my heart in half like when I heard Mom say she only wanted money. Somehow, Mrs. Parker's words feel like the kiss I'd get on an owie from Dad when I was younger. The hurt is still there, but somehow I know the pain will go away.

"I love you too, Mrs. Parker."

She chuckles. "Just call me Regina."

"Okay." My tears are drying up, and I can take in a full breath now. "Thank you. Thank you for being kind to me."

"Oh, sweetie, being kind to you is the easiest thing in the world."

I'm grinning now. I'm not sure why my own mom doesn't want me, but maybe it's not about me. Because Mrs. Parker—Regina—does love me, and Dad loves me and RJ and Kyleigh and . . . I'm not sure who else, but people *do* love me. And Dad said God loves me even more than he does, so, yeah, maybe it's not about me but Mom.

"Do you want to talk to Kyleigh again?"

"Yes, please."

"All right, you call me if you ever need to talk. Okay?"

"I will."

When Kyleigh gets back on the phone, I tell her a truth I hope she knows. "Your mom is the best."

"I know I'm lucky. And I'm sorry your mom is the way she is."

I snort. "Me too. It stinks we have to go skiing with her."

Kyleigh gasps. "I completely forgot about that. What are we going to do?"

"Make her wish she didn't come?" I wince. My dad would *not* like that attitude, but I still can't believe Mom's been faking nice for money.

"Like on *The Parent Trap* movies."

My mouth drops. How did I forget? "Yes!" I breathe out. "Exactly like that."

Maybe going on the ski trip this year won't be such a bad thing after all.

Chapter *eighteen*

Kyleigh

"Are we really doing this?" I ask.

I glance at Malea's mom, standing near her dad. She's got her fake hair up in a high ponytail and designer ski clothes, but I can see a tag hanging from her jacket. She's probably trying to show off so we'll like her—which won't work. But does that mean we should be mean to her like she was mean to Malea and Theo?

"Definitely. She can't come here and treat me or Dad like this." Malea frowns. "Plus, she did something to your mom. I don't know what, but I don't like it."

I straighten to my full height. No one messes with my best friend *or* Mom. "Then let's do this. We can't do the stuff from the movies. She's old, she probably saw it when it originally came out."

Malea nods. "Right."

"Okay, first up, this." I hold up two powder packets.

"We're adding flavor to her water?" Malea asks skeptically.

I grin, letting out a menacing laugh and rubbing my hands with glee. "It's laxative powder. My mom's given them to me before. Usually she uses one, but I think two would have her running to the bathroom."

Malea laughs. "You're diabolical."

I frown. "What's that mean?"

She shrugs. "I heard it on a video. I'm guessing it means *bad*."

"In this case, you're probably right. I also brought these." I hold up my pack of tiny Christmas ornaments. "We can put them under the sheets in her bed."

"At least it's not under her window." Malea smirks and I giggle. "Do you think that's enough, or do you have more?"

"In the movie, the twins try to scare the stepmom with wildlife, but we'll be in a resort." Malea showed me pictures of her trip last year, and the place looks amazing. I can't wait to see it myself. I'm not sure how I'll survive the bunny slopes, but Malea assures me I'll have fun.

"Then I guess this is enough."

We walk to Mr. Evers's truck and get in the back seat.

"Sit in the middle," Malea says. "RJ's coming with us."

"Oh, cool!" I wish my mom would too, but she kept telling me that Malea needs this time with her mom. Little does she know we'll make sure her mom stays away for good and never hurts Malea again.

Soon the adults all get in the car, and we're off.

I'm a little nervous. I've never been on a ski trip, and I'm not sure just these two ideas will have Malea's mom running away like that evil stepmom wannabe in the movies. What was her name again? *Meredith! That's right.*

We get to the resort faster than I guessed. I stare at the

building, gaping at the number of windows and the snow surrounding the area. I grab my bag, and RJ and Mr. Evers grab their stuff.

"Get your mom's water," I whisper to Malea.

"Right." She heads over to her mom and is all smiles. Give that girl an Oscar. She should be an actress.

Malea offers to help her mom carry stuff and takes the water bottle, acting normal the entire time. While her mom struggles to pick up all her luggage, we add the powder packets to her drink.

The walk to the resort lobby and then to our rooms is uneventful. No lizard to put on her water bottle. No rocks to add to her cross-body purse. The one bad thing . . . Malea and I are sharing a room with her. Malea places the water bottle on the nightstand next to the bed her mom chose.

"I'm going to shower off the grime from the ride." She waves a hand in the air. "Do something."

Malea and I grin at each other. As soon as the bathroom door closes, I place the ornaments under her pillow and sheets. A knock sounds at the door, and we freeze.

"Malea, it's your dad."

"Phew," she mumbles.

We straighten the comforter, then Malea opens the door.

"You two ready for some food?"

"Yes!" we chime together, then giggle.

"Where's your mom?"

"In the shower." Malea barely stops from rolling her eyes.

"Let her know to meet us in the restaurant, then come out in the hall."

"Okay, Dad."

We're seated at a table for five. The mood is festive and not awkward at all because Malea's mom hasn't arrived. RJ orders some fish dish, Theo gets a steak, Malea gets chicken tenders, and I get spaghetti.

Mrs. Evers—is she still Mrs. Evers?—arrives after we placed our orders.

She huffs in irritation. “You didn’t wait to see what I wanted?”

“Oh, no worries. I ordered you fish,” RJ jokes.

Her nose wrinkles. “I don’t eat that.” She flags the waiter down and assures him she doesn’t want the fish and orders a plate of spaghetti like me.

Bruh!

Malea nudges me, and I look up to see her mom take a long swig of water. Oh man, everything is going according to plan. How long will it take for the laxative to kick in? Mom only gives me one, and usually by the end of the day, I’m in the bathroom. I can only hope two packs is enough to get something happening before we finish dinner. It’s actually a long walk from the rooms to the restaurant. I’m not sure if I saw any bathrooms in the lobby.

Finally, our food arrives, and we all dive in.

“How’s your room?” Theo asks.

“It was a little chilly, and the shower didn’t get that hot, but it’ll do,” Malea’s mom complains.

Malea narrows her eyes and, when the adults are distracted, adds pepper to Mrs. Evers’s spaghetti. My mouth drops. That’s genius!

Mrs. Evers frowns after taking her next bite. “This is so peppery. What were they thinking?” She turns to stare at me. “How’s your spaghetti?”

“Perfect.” I smile, hoping it looks innocent, but I’m trying not to laugh.

"Such a subpar place." She grabs her water bottle and takes a long swallow.

Malea and I grin at each other. Let the fun begin!

Theo

I grab the items to make s'mores, then RJ and I head across the hall to get the girls. The resort has public firepits outdoors, and I promised Malea and Kyleigh s'mores if they ate all their dinner. Unfortunately, Jianna didn't finish hers, but I can't police a grown woman.

The door opens, and Jianna grimaces. "S'mores?"

"The girls are excited about them."

She places a hand on her stomach. "I don't think I want to come."

"You're supposed to be here for our daughter," I whisper. I have no idea if Malea can hear, but I'll do my best to ensure she doesn't.

"Fine, but I'm not eating those."

"Then don't," I snap. Really, why does she have to make everything so difficult?

We head out to the firepit, and I show Kyleigh how to make the s'more since she said Regina has never made them for her before.

"This is amazing!" Kyleigh says after taking a bite.

"I'll send you home with some of the fixings, so you two can make them together. G loves s'mores."

RJ nods. "Sure does. She always used to try and eat ours too."

I laugh at the memory.

"What's so funny about that?" Jianna asks snidely.

Ugh, I can't wait for Cruella to leave. But I force a smile to my face. I don't want Malea to know how irritated I am with her mom. "Not sure you'd understand." I hold up a graham cracker. "Sure you don't want any?"

Her lips purse. "They're not all that."

"How can you say that?" Malea looks shocked.

I'm not sure if she's genuinely horrified or pretending to be. Since Jianna came over the other day, Malea's been acting weird. If I didn't know better, I'd think she heard our conversation about her mom not coming to Holly for her. Surely that would've made her cry if she *did* eavesdrop. But I haven't seen a single teardrop.

"Oh, Malea, honey, Mommy doesn't look this way because I eat all that sugar. If you want to grow up to look like me, you'll make sure that's the last one you eat."

My spine snaps straight, and my teeth clench so hard I'm surprised I don't feel shards shatter from the action. "Don't talk to her like that. There's nothing wrong with the way she looks."

Jianna blinks at me, then glances at our daughter. "I mean, of course not. She's not overweight or anything, but sugar is so bad for your health."

Can I point out that the hair on Jianna's head isn't hers and that face she's wearing was helped by cosmetics? Jianna is faker than a two-dollar bill. She has no room to talk, and I don't want my daughter thinking she has to alter herself just to be beautiful. She's perfect as is.

Don't argue in front of the girls or insult Jianna in front of them. Exercise your self-control. I drag in an inhale. *Lord God, shut my mouth and give me grace, please. I don't want to lose it.*

My insides are already simmering close to the edge, so I purposely take a big bite of the chocolate confection and give the loudest "Mmm" possible. Jianna looks away with disgust, but the smirk on RJ's face and the joy on the girls' faces means I don't care one iota what my ex thinks.

"Water is so much better." She grabs her water bottle and takes a long swig.

The girls giggle, and I arch a brow at their reaction. Granted, no kid wants to drink water, but I don't think that choice is that funny either.

"Though this water does taste a little strange."

RJ frowns. "Why? Is your water bottle dirty? When's the last time you cleaned it?"

"I'm not dirty, RJ. I cleaned it last night." She sucks her teeth. "Probably shouldn't have used that nasty tap water at Theo's place. He needs a filter."

I already have one installed in the house. Got it after she left, but she doesn't need to know that. I give a discreet shake of the head, so RJ doesn't say anything. He roasts a marshmallow, then stuffs it in his mouth.

Guess I'm not the only one trying to stay out of trouble by having a mouth full of food all the time.

"Dad, you should sing us a song," Malea says.

"Yes." Kyleigh claps. "Let's all sing."

"If you're going to sing, I'm going to bed. I don't want to hear that noise."

The girls exchange looks but say nothing.

"But you love to sing," I point out. Jianna's acting like a brat, but she grabs her stomach again, so maybe she has a reason for being in a foul mood.

"Professionally, not with amateurs."

Kyleigh frowns, but Malea whispers in her ear, and her face relaxes.

"Fine. Good night."

She rushes away. As soon as Jianna's out of earshot, I look at my daughter. "I'm sure you'll get time with your mom tomorrow."

Malea shrugs as if she doesn't care, but how can she not? Having Jianna around is all she's ever wanted.

"You okay?" I ask.

"Yeah, Dad, I'm great." She loops an arm through Kyleigh's, and they smile at each other.

A sense of foreboding slides down my spine. That smile is almost identical to her plotting face when she was trying to get Regina and me together.

I narrow my gaze at my daughter. "What did you do?"

Chapter *nineteen*

Theo

I knock on the door to Regina's house. The girls are standing in front of me because I'm not letting them out of my sight.

The door swings open, and Kris blinks in surprise.

"G home?" I ask.

"Yeah, come on in." She moves away from the door, allowing us to cross the threshold. "I'll go get her."

"Thanks." I motion to the couch. "You two sit. Not a word out of your mouths."

Regina walks into the room wearing a hoodie and sweatpants. I want to pull her into my arms, but instead, I fold them across my chest. Stern Dad is in the building, and I can't let my guard down and let these girls think I'm okay with their actions.

"What happened?" Regina says breathlessly.

"Why don't I let them share the news." I motion for them to go ahead.

Malea sighs. "Well, um, you know how I overheard my mom?"

"Wait, what?" They didn't tell me this part. "You heard us talking?"

Malea nods.

I squeeze the bridge of my nose. That certainly sheds a new light on things.

"Continue," Regina says softly, sinking into a chair catty-corner from the couch.

"She also said she tried to mess up your relationship with Dad. I was mad. I wanted to show my mom she can't treat people like that. So we came up with a plan."

"Both of you?" Regina asks.

The girls nod.

"What was the plan?" Regina stares at Kyleigh.

"Um, I brought some laxative powder to put in Malea's mom's water and tiny ornaments to put under her sheets."

Regina's mouth drops open. Yep, same expression I had when they spilled the beans.

I take over the story. "They also put pepper on her dinner, which of course meant she drank more of her water. When she rushed toward her room, the girls exchanged a look. That's when I knew they were up to something," I add.

Apparently, Jianna barely made it to the bathroom, and afterward, all she wanted to do was lie down. And found the ornaments. She demanded we take her back to Holly immediately. We barely made it to the B and B parking lot before she hopped out of the car to race to the bathroom once again.

"You didn't." Regina sounds aghast.

"We're sorry," the girls say in unison.

G looks at me, and I stare back. *What do we do?* I mouth.

"Girls, go to Kyleigh's room so I can talk with Theo."

"Don't turn on the TV," I say.

"Or use your cell phones," Regina adds.

"Yes, ma'am," Kyleigh mumbles.

"Yes, sir." Malea lowers her head and follows Kyleigh out of the room.

"Are they really that contrite, or are they faking?" she asks after a few moments.

I sink onto the couch. "I have no idea." I rub the back of my neck.

We need to talk about the girls and the fiasco of the trip, but more than that, I want to know where Regina and I stand. The last time we talked, I left unsure of whether we're still in a relationship or not. But the girls . . .

"Obviously they shouldn't get any use of electronics," Regina states.

"Agreed."

She bites her lip, and I glance away so I'm not distracted.

"Did Malea tell you we talked?" she asks softly.

I face Regina. "About the conversation she overheard?"

She nods.

"How much did she hear?"

"All of it."

I groan. No wonder she was so upset. "But to put laxative powder in her drink?"

"That little girl was abandoned, Theo. And we've gotten close enough that she took exception to her mother trying to sabotage our relationship."

I perk up. Does that mean we still have a relationship?

Dude, focus on one thing at a time. Focus on your daughter.

"Are you saying I should be lenient?"

"Compassionate," Regina counters. "I can't imagine the hurt she's experienced or the doubt she has about if she's loveable or not. So when she realized the one person who's supposed to love her above all else just wanted money . . ." Her voice trails off. "She reacted. It's our—I mean *your*—job to help her deal with the emotions."

I cannot keep this slaphappy expression off my face.

"What?" Regina folds her arms across her chest. "Why are you staring at me like that?"

"You said 'our job.'"

"Nope." She shakes her head. "Your job. You're her dad. I'm just . . ."

"Just what?" I arch a brow. "My girlfriend?"

She bites her lip. "I want to be."

Yes! Thank You, Lord. "Then having space while we were gone helped?" It's not the real question I want to ask, but the smarter one.

"Oh, because you were gone so long." She smirks.

"Hey, don't blame me. That's Kyleigh who's lacing people's water." I chuckle and shake my head. "I shouldn't laugh. I'm still horrified. But my word, where did she even get that idea?"

"Those tiny ornaments have to be a Kevin McCallister nod. Maybe watching that before you guys left wasn't the smartest idea."

"You think? I'm told Jianna screamed like someone held her at gunpoint."

Regina's jaw drops. "Really? Who told you that?"

"Concierge."

She squeezes her eyes and shakes her head. "Our children are menaces, or your ex-wife is the pea princess."

I snort. "She's no princess. Anyone would feel ornaments

under their pillow and sheets. And our children are definitely menaces." But I love that they wanted to protect Regina, though I wish they had just *talked* to me instead.

"Is she going to stay in Holly?" Regina asks.

"No. She told me she shouldn't have wasted her time trying to get money from me when she could find any number of guys willing to provide for her in Nashville."

Regina glances toward the hall, then meets my gaze. "How does Malea feel about that?"

"She said, 'Dingdong the witch is gone.'"

G's eyes widen to abnormal proportions, then a burst of laughter escapes. "Not funny, but funny."

I sigh. If we can't even keep ourselves collected, how can we effectively discipline our children? But after a few more seconds, I give in to the laughter and release the tension that's been in my body since my ex-wife walked into the sundae shop.

Regina

I know my laughter is slightly unhinged, but being home without Kyleigh and knowing they were all skiing without me gave me a *lot* of time and space to think. I realized how much I wanted a relationship with Theo and didn't want anyone to keep me from him, especially my own self. I've done so much to silence myself, and after getting to the point where I can sing and try out for the church worship team, I don't want to go backward.

Never did I imagine Theo and the girls would return early because the girls keep living out their Lindsay Lohan dreams. I can't believe that movie has been out more than twenty-five years, and the original, well, I don't want to count that far back. I mean, I wasn't alive for the premiere, but I've seen one, two, three, *and* four, plus the Lindsay Lohan remake.

Stay on topic. Having my daughter gone and knowing she was with Theo seemed to break down the barriers I couldn't when he was right in front of me. Even now, I want to go to him and hug him while promising to never let go. Instead, I ask what our plan is before bringing the girls back to the living room.

These two seriously need to be disciplined for their actions. They can't go around enacting vengeance on people, especially on Malea's own mother. The thought is sobering, and I say a prayer for God to guide Theo and me. Then I yell for the girls.

Kyleigh and Malea shuffle into the living room, looking like the most downtrodden children I have ever laid eyes on. Maybe they actually do feel remorseful. I'm not sure, considering my own feelings are torn. Yet I'm glad Jianna won't be causing any more problems. Theo and Malea don't deserve her—*at all*. However, I'm appalled the girls took action on their own accord.

"What do you think your punishment should be?" Theo asks the girls.

They exchange glances, surprise all over their faces.

"Um," Malea finally speaks. "No phone use."

"Oh, that's a given," I interject. "But I'm interested to hear how long you think that rule should be in effect."

Kyleigh's face blanches. *Yep!* That girl's attached to her phone, so I know she'll lowball the offer. The girls whisper to one another.

"Three days?" Malea questions.

Theo and I were thinking the same so that's easy.

"Done. What else?" Theo says.

Kyleigh lets out a pitiful whimper. Homegirl is delusional if she thinks a lack of a cell phone is the only consequence for trying to mess with an adult. I've always taught her to respect her elders, even if they don't return that respect. Respect is part of loving like God commands us to do.

"No streaming for the same amount of time," Kyleigh suggests.

"Fine." Theo looks at the girls. "Do you have anything you want to say?"

Kyleigh bites her lips and looks at Theo, then me. "I'm sorry. I shouldn't have come up with the ideas. I thought it would be harmless but also annoying enough to show Malea deserved better. But I know what we—what *I*—did was wrong."

"I should've told you what I heard instead of trying to hurt Mom like she hurt me." Malea sniffs. "She hurt my feelings, but I tried to hurt her physically."

Theo opens his arms, and Malea rushes into them. My heart breaks for the turmoil she's been through. Although I disagree with her methods, I understand that knee-jerk reaction. I should've done more to ensure she was okay when she called before the trip.

After a moment, Malea pulls back from Theo, and I open my arms. She almost knocks me over, thankfully the couch stops the momentum. I wrap my arms around her and whisper in her ear.

"I love you. Don't feel like you have to defend yourself. You know your dad and I will be there for you. And God is our defense." Even if Theo and I don't work out, I vow to be in Malea's life as long as she'll have me.

"I love you too," she whispers, squeezing me even tighter.

My heart melts, and I open my left arm for Kyleigh to join us. She nestles in my lap next to Malea, and I let out a sigh. Somehow Malea has burrowed herself into my heart. Seeing my own child trying to defend her BFF shows me just how close these two have grown over the school year.

Theo goes into the kitchen and starts rummaging around in my fridge. I know we have to have our own discussion, but I'm thankful he's not pushing the issue right now.

Soon food is being cooked, the girls are setting the table, and I'm dragging Kris out of her room to join us.

"Look, y'all need this family time."

I roll my eyes. "Like you're not part of the family. Come out of your cave and join civilization."

"Fine."

Kris pads down the hall after me. We enter the kitchen area, and Theo smiles at me.

"It's almost finished."

"Need any help?" I ask.

"Want to make a salad?"

Not particularly. Vegetables are my kryptonite, but I am always telling Kyleigh she needs more greens. Guess I should lead by example.

Kris grabs drinks for everyone while I make the salad. Then, Theo's putting the finished pasta in a serving bowl and placing it in the middle of my dining table. I glance around the table. It's never been this full. I study Kyleigh to see how she's feeling about it. Her eyes are bright, and she shares a smile with me.

As I look around the table at my family, I realize this is exactly what Kyleigh hoped for and what I've been too afraid to pray for.

Thank You, Lord, for knowing what I needed before I even figured it out. Thank You for Kyleigh and the joy she's brought in my life and for opening our hearts to new possibilities. I'm not sure what will happen between me and Theo, but I know Your plans are good. I trust You no matter what.

Chapter *twenty*

Regina

After supper, I grab the throw blanket and my beanie and follow Theo to the front porch. He wants to talk, and my nerves are attempting to twist my insides like a gymnast doing a flip in the air. I settle on the chair, wrapping my body with the blanket to ward off the dipping temperatures that prove we're firmly in winter.

"How are you handling everything?" I ask when the silence goes on far too long.

"For Malea's sake, I toned down just how mad Jianna was." He sighs and leans back against the chair. "I doubt we'll see her for a long time."

I wince. "Do you think Malea will be okay with that? I mean, I know she ran her off, but was that the hurt talking, or does she really not want her around?"

"Probably a little bit from column A and column B."

Oof. "Now what?"

"Now we talk about us and not my ex."

My face heats. I know this is why we came outside, but I'm worried, nonetheless. "Okay."

"Let's talk about trust," Theo starts.

"I'm sorry," I blurb out. I don't know what else he plans on saying, but I need to get it out while I can because he deserves an apology.

"G . . ." His face softens, and he cups my cheek. "I didn't bring you out here for an apology or for you to think I'm mad. I just want to make sure we're communicating. For you to know how much you mean to me and that I'm okay going at your pace."

"Yeah, but I insinuated I wasn't trusting you even though I said it wasn't about trusting you. Regardless of the situation, I didn't trust you with my heart, and I'm sorry. You did nothing to deserve that." A pricking sensation pokes at my eyelids, but I need to maintain my calm and gaze into Theo's handsome face. I don't want to miss a single moment of this conversation.

"I know you've been hurt, G. I know life has knocked you down a few times. I'm not asking you to trust in this one hundred percent just yet because we haven't been on but one date. Understand?"

I nod. Because I do. He's being Theo all over again. Telling me he's for me, that he'll go at my pace because he knows that's what I need. Theo has always looked out for my best interest. Why didn't I remember that when we were teenagers? Why didn't I trust that we would've figured out a way to be together even if I pursued a career on Broadway?

"Listen," he starts again. "I *do* need you to know that my endgame is me, you, and the girls for a lifetime. So while I know we're new-ish, I'm also not wasting this second chance. I fully believe we'll fall in love again, like we did when we were kids. I fully believe that one day, I'll get down on one knee."

Tears spill over at his sincerity. I don't know how this man can wear his heart on his sleeve after I broke his heart and then Jianna stomped all over it, but I'm more than thankful that heartache didn't change who he is at his core.

I want to tell him how I feel, but the words are trapped in my heart, and my lips aren't allowing one word to pass by. Instead, I wrap my arms around his neck and pull him to me. That Christmas tree farm smell envelops me, and the ache that's been in my chest since Jianna showed up dissipates. Peace fills my heart, and I know I'm home in his arms.

Theo softly brushes my lips with his. Warmth encompasses me as he lets me know how he feels about me, about us, and our future. I match each expression of affection with my own until we sit back, breath uneven but hearts full.

"Then it's official? You're my girlfriend?" Theo asks.

I smile at him. "Yes, boyfriend."

He throws a fist in the air, and I'm giggling like a teen all over again. There's something about Theo Evers that makes me feel young and in love. Though I'm not ready to say so out loud, I can admit it to myself. The giddiness is effervescent and makes me want to float down the sidewalk, surrounded by all the Christmas décor and lights. It's like the season has perfectly captured how I feel.

"Will you, Kyleigh, and Kris celebrate Christmas with us?"

"Yes." I don't have to think, don't have to question. I will be at his house bright and early, wearing pjs and carrying gifts like my address resides at the North Pole.

He leans over and kisses me once more. "Can't wait."

"Neither can I."

And I truly can't. This has been the best holiday of my

adult life yet. But if Kyleigh asks, I'll tone down my happiness so she doesn't think she's right. I cannot let a ten-year-old develop an ego this early in the game. I still have to survive her teenage years, but something tells me I won't be alone when they come.

Theo

CHRISTMAS DAY

"I haven't seen you this adrenaline filled in a long time. You know she already likes you, right? I doubt G expected you to go all out."

I ignore RJ and continue icing the cinnamon rolls. "She's not the only one coming over."

RJ huffs. "I don't count."

"Look, man." I stand up straight, icing bag in hand. "She invited her parents."

The laughter builds in RJ's body before it makes it out of his mouth, but when it does, the sound is long and loud. I ignore him until every single cinnamon roll has been frosted and is ready to go out on the dining table.

The doorbell chimes, and RJ takes a sip of his coffee. I cock my head, and he shakes his.

"Not my circus. There's a reason I don't date."

I scoff. "Mark my words, I'll be doing the laughing next Christmas."

"In your dreams, bro."

"Nah, son, my prayers." I smirk and head toward the front door. "In my daily prayers," I call over my shoulder.

"You're praying for what?" Malea asks as she meets me at the door.

"RJ to find a wife."

She grins and rubs her hands with glee. "I've been praying for that too. God's listening because it's two of us, right?"

I love my daughter. I love the innocence in her expression, the self-assurance that God's listening no matter what. This season, she's taught me to hope like I never have before.

"That's right." I lean down and kiss her forehead, then motion for her to open the door.

"Kyleigh!" Malea jumps up and down as if she didn't just see her best friend last night.

"Squirt, back up so they can get in the house. It's cold outside."

"Oh, right." She gives Kyleigh a sheepish expression.

I kiss Regina on the cheek and grab the bundle of gifts from her. "Wow, you went all out," I murmur.

"You know giving gifts makes me happy."

The smile on her face softens my insides. Because I do know she loves to give gifts. G was always trying to find some reason to do so when we were growing up together and even more so when we started dating. I'm so happy she can mention the past and not linger on regrets any longer.

"I do. I hope you like receiving them too." Why didn't I hang up mistletoe in my house?

"What did you get me?" An eager expression appears on her face.

"Guess you'll have to wait and see when we open presents."

Her face falls into a pout, and I can't help myself. I kiss her soft lips, then back away. "Let's go get ready to eat. Your parents still coming?"

"Yeah, they should be here soon." She glances at her watch.

Someone knocks on the door. "Bet that's them." She turns around and opens the door.

My arms are still full of the gifts, so I dash to the living room and quickly go back to the doorway to welcome her folks in.

Soon we're all around the dining table eating cinnamon rolls, fruit, and the quiche Regina's mom made for us. I can't remember the last time my house was this full. It's giving me life, and I hope it's a sign of things to come.

After we finish breakfast, we mosey into the living room. Kris and RJ take the love seat, the girls choose to sit right in front of the Christmas tree while the rest of us squeeze onto the couch. I pull Regina as close as possible and drape my arm around her shoulder. She snuggles into me and a welling of thanks pours out. *You are amazing, Lord. Thank You for today.*

Who would've thought I'd get a chance to right the one regret I had? As laughter springs around us, and the girls start opening gifts, my gaze can't help but lock on to Regina.

"Stop staring," she whispers out of the side of her mouth. "My folks are here and so are the girls."

"I'm just admiring your beauty. I'm not doing anything naughty."

She huffs. "You're melting the side of my face with your stare."

"You like it."

She kisses my cheek, then turns my head forward. "I do, but let's exchange looks later. Right now you're missing the gifts."

"Fine."

It's a good thing I focus because Kyleigh just opened the present Malea bought with her allowance. It's a best-friends-forever necklace that breaks perfectly in half.

"This is peak!" Kyleigh exclaims. "It almost matches mine." Kyleigh grabs a gift under the tree and hands it to Malea. "Open!"

Malea grins as she rips the paper open. Her mouth drops when she opens the jewelry box. "Dad, look!" Malea races to me and shows me a necklace that has two connecting puzzle pieces. One piece has a *K* and the other an *M*.

"Wow, squirt. That's amazing."

She nods, then goes back to the mountain of wrapping paper piling up on the floor.

"Be right back." I find a trash bag to stuff some of the remnants into, then set it next to the couch.

Regina's parents bought gifts for both of the girls. They give Malea a sweater in her favorite color and Kyleigh one in hers. They even hand out gifts for me and RJ. I can tell from the surprise lining his forehead that the gift is unexpected and welcomed.

I hand Regina her two gifts. I bought one in case she decides the homemade one is terrible. I hand her the homemade one first. "Open, please."

She gives me an amused glance but unwraps the package slowly. I forgot how meticulous she is with wrapping paper. She probably has a place in her house where all the old wrapping paper goes to live for a second chance at being opened. After what seems like forever, she opens the box.

"You bought me a candle?" She stares quizzically at the round jar.

"No, I *made* you a candle. Kyleigh taught me how."

Her eyes well up, and she opens it, inhaling dramatically. "Oh my goodness. Why does that smell so good?" She glances at the candle and *finally* reads what I typed up for a label: *Smells like family.*

"Theo . . ." she whispers.

"Is that okay?"

"I love it."

Thank-yous go all around, and when we're done, we watch *The Chosen*'s Christmas episode about the birth of Jesus.

When Regina's parents make their exit, and RJ offers Kris a ride home, I know it's only a matter of time before Regina and Kyleigh leave. However, I'm not saying good-bye to Regina forever. We're committed to one another, to our daughters, and to the future God has for us.

Later, after I walk Regina to her car, I hug her close.

"Merry Christmas, beautiful," I say.

"Merry Christmas, Theo."

I brush my lips against hers, mindful to keep the kiss rated G since her daughter is waiting in the car and mine is probably peeking from the doorway. One day, I hope that I won't have to kiss Regina good-bye and see her leave but instead kiss her good night and wake up to her the next day.

Epilogue

Malea

NEW YEAR'S EVE

When I prayed that God would give me a mom, I assumed it wouldn't be my own mom. Since Mom went back to Nashville, she hasn't reached out. It's sad but also my reality. But now that Regina is in my life, I'm happier than ever. When Kyleigh and I decided to trap our parents into a relationship, it was the best idea we could've ever come up with. I'm not sure why they broke up in high school, but I'm thankful they found each other again. I think they're perfect for each other.

Dad whistles around the house now and hasn't been out to the chopping block since Mom's brief visit. Regina is over at our house almost every day, which means I get to see Kyleigh as well. We tried to get our parents to propose already, but they claim they need time to date and get reacquainted.

I'm not sure why because they've known each other since kindergarten or something like that. Even I know Regina will be my mom one day. But if they feel the need to pretend like it isn't inevitable, fine.

I look at the stars on my ceiling. "Do you think they're still dancing?" I ask Kyleigh.

"Definitely. All they do is find excuses to hug or kiss." She sighs. "They're so romantic."

"How long do you think it'll take for them to propose?"

Kyleigh groans. "I have no idea. I don't know why your dad didn't on Christmas. I told him it was okay with me."

"Same. I told him to do it for New Year's too."

"We could ring in the new year as a family, right?" Kyleigh props her chin on her hand.

"Definitely. They're delaying our future happiness . . . for what?"

"Probably so they don't have to admit we were right."

I laugh. "They're so silly. Don't they know we'll just make plans to get them to propose sooner?"

"I don't know, Malea. The last time we made plans to interfere with grown-up business, we got in trouble."

I frown. Kyleigh's not wrong, but they're taking forever. "Don't you want to be a family already? I mean, there's obviously enough room in here for you to sleep." I turn over in my twin bed and glance at Kyleigh in the trundle bed. "Or if you wanted, we could turn Dad's office into your room."

She shrugs. "I don't care as long as we all live together like a real family."

"Then see, we need to come up with a plan to get them to propose sooner. We can't wait until next Christmas to see them get their act together."

Kyleigh shudders. "All right, fine." She smiles. "What are you thinking?"

Kyleigh

MARCH

I shush Malea as we make our way through the tree farm. If she keeps yapping, she'll give away our position and ruin stealth mode.

"But I think we're going the wrong way," she whispers.

I pause and glance around me. Although Theo has been teaching me and Malea what goes into caring for the trees that aren't ready to sell, I sometimes get lost walking through the farm. *All the trees look alike!*

Maybe Malea was right to speak up. "Do you know where we are?" I ask her.

Malea looks around, then smiles. "Yes. We have to go that way." She points to the right, so I turn and follow her lead.

After a while her steps slow, and she motions for me to be quiet. I roll my eyes because the only one who's been talking this whole time is her. We peek around one of the trees and watch as our parents sit in a clearing.

Mom's black hair is full of curls that Kris did. She thinks she's on a regular date, but we know better. Our plan to get our parents engaged is finally coming together. Malea and I both agreed to say how often we liked each other's parent to our own parent in hopes they would realize we needed to be a family sooner rather than later.

I also made sure to say how happy my mom was around Theo and that it must be love. She hadn't said she loved him until one day she came home looking giddy and told me they were in love. If it weren't for me and Malea, they'd still be talking about needing time to get reacquainted.

Adults.

Theo turns on his cell phone and Taylor Swift plays.

"It's happening," Malea whispers.

I place a finger over my lips and give her a warning glare. But inside, I'm just as happy. I can't wait to be a family and live on the tree farm forever.

After the song comes to an end, Theo gets down on one knee. Tears appear out of nowhere, and I slip a hand over my mouth to keep silent. I don't want to ruin this for Mom. Malea reaches over and grabs my other hand. I glance at her and see she has tears going down her face as well.

We both face forward in time to hear Mom say, "Yes, I'll marry you!"

They wrap each other in a hug and kiss. I look away to give them privacy and smile at Malea.

"We did it," I whisper.

"We're officially sisters!" she says.

I'm not sure how long we stand there grinning, but when we snap to, we do our handshake before turning back down the lane toward her house—*our* future house—hand in hand.

Discussion Questions

1. Have you ever matched two people? If so, how did it go? If not, which two people would you pick to matchmake and why?

2. What does the Christmas season mean to you?

3. The Christmas season can be difficult for some people, as is evident in the character of Kris. How can you include others during this time?

4. Which character stole the show for you and how?

5. Which character did you relate to the most and why?

6. What's one line you underlined or that's been repeating in your mind?

7. Regina was worried that Jianna's reappearance meant she'd have to give up her relationship with

Theo. Do you agree with Theo's response to her fears? Why or why not?

8. Theo tries his best to get Malea to see all that matters is that she's loved by God. Do you believe this for yourself? Why or why not?

9. This story has themes of second chances and hoping in God. Which theme impacted you the most and why?

10. What surprised you most about the book? Did you feel there were any significant plot twists? If so, what were they?

Acknowledgments

Another book is done! I can't believe how fast this book (the first draft) came together, but I have also loved seeing it go through its many stages. You know what they say: When you give an author a story idea, you have to thank the people who helped along the way.

Thanks to my agent extraordinaire, who helped me get a two-book Christmas contract. This idea made me positively giddy, and I thank you for championing me! You're the best agent, Rachel McMillian.

Next I'd love to thank Carrie Schmidt for reading this story in its early stages and encouraging me. Your friendship is something I deeply treasure. Thank you for all you do!

A special thank you to Katie Combs for the candle shop name! I adore it and wish it were a real place!

I'd also like to thank David Swift, Erich Kästner, and Nancy Meyers, among others, for fueling my love for all things *The Parent Trap*. I also had the best time infusing my love of Christmas with the iconic movies!

Many thanks to my readers. Your enthusiasm for my books, encouraging emails, etc., make this author journey a blessing. I may never meet you in person, but you hold a special place in my heart and in my prayers. I hope you loved this book as much as I did writing it.

Last, but certainly not least, many thanks to my husband and children. Thank you for putting up with my Christmas music during the summer. Thanks, Isaiah, for recommending songs for my playlist. Elijah, thanks for listening to me brainstorm out loud and being a sounding board. Glenn, even though I may blush whenever you're telling random strangers I'm an author, it means the world to me. You guys are my joy and the reason I can write happily-ever-after books. I love you!

For more Christmas love stories from
Toni Shiloh, check out

You Make It Feel like Christmas

and

The Christmas Catch

* * * *

And Coming Soon:

Look for Kris's sweet holiday romance, available September 2027.

* * * *

Toni Shiloh is a wife, a mom, and an award-winning Christian contemporary romance author. She writes to bring God glory and to learn more about His goodness. Her novel *In Search of a Prince* won the first ever Christy Amplify Award. Her books have won the Selah Award and have been finalists for the Carol Award and the HOLT Medallion. A member of American Christian Fiction Writers (ACFW), Toni loves connecting with readers and authors alike via social media. You can learn more about her writing at ToniShiloh.com.

Sign Up for Toni's Newsletter

Keep up to date with Toni's latest news on book releases and events by signing up for her email list at the website below.

ToniShiloh.com

FOLLOW TONI ON SOCIAL MEDIA

Toni Shiloh, Author

@ToniShiloh

@ToniShilohWrite